Nathan Goodman

Breach of Protocol

THOUGHT REACH PRESS, a publishing division of Thought Reach, LLC. United States of America.

First Thought Reach Press printing January, 2017
ISBN: 978-1540470812
Printed in the USA and United Kingdom.

For information regarding special discounts for bulk purchases, or permission to reproduce any content other than mentioned above, contact the publisher at
support@thoughtreach.com.

Other novels in The Jana Baker Spy-Thriller Series, by
Nathan Goodman

The Fourteenth Protocol

Protocol 15

**Get a free copy of Book 1 of this series, *The Fourteenth
Protocol*, by visiting** NathanAGoodman.com/fourteen/

I

Part One

1

A COLD VOICE

The Camino trail, western Spain. About one mile from the town of Melide.

There's not much of a cell signal along the Camino de Santiago, a five-hundred-mile trail known as *The Way of Saint James*, that runs through Spain's rural countryside. So when the phone vibrated, it startled Jana. It had been her habit to leave the phone off until she found a hostel to sleep for the night. As it was, she was high on a bluff near Melide, just two days' hike from the town of Santiago de Compostela, terminus of the Camino trail.

"We have a cell signal up here? Hang on," she said to Gilda, a fortysomething hiker from Berlin she had befriended on the trail. "I thought this thing was turned off."

"Probably that boyfriend of yours," Gilda teased. "And don't forget, it's your turn to buy the wine tonight."

"Oh no. Last time I did that, you got hammered."

"Me?" Gilda laughed. "You were singing karaoke in Spanish, and you don't speak Spanish."

Jana laughed as she fished in her backpack for the phone. "Oh yeah. What was it you said I told the waiter? That I wanted to sleep with him?"

"Took a while to convince him you didn't exactly have a command of the language."

Jana looked at the phone. The caller ID said "Unknown."

"Yeah, must be Cade calling me from his work," she said. "But why would he not just use his cell phone?"

"He probably found out you made a pass at that waiter," Gilda said with a smile.

"Remind me to smack you later."

"Hello," Jana said into the phone, but the only thing she could hear was the hollow sound of someone breathing. She looked across the surrounding hillsides, unsure why her nerves were suddenly on edge.

"Enjoying your little walk, *Agent* Baker?" a cold Middle Eastern voice said.

Ice raced into Jana's bloodstream and her mind locked.

"Who is this?"

"Oh, but, Miss Baker," the man said, his throat raspy and deep. "I would have thought you people would have my voice memorized by now."

Her eyes scanned the horizon as if they might uncover someone watching.

Gilda put her hand on Jana's arm. "Is everything okay?"

Jana stepped away and continued to look in all directions.

"I asked who this was."

"Oh, I think you know," the man said through a laugh. "Say it. Say my name, Miss Baker."

A wave of terror leaked into Jana's veins as she grabbed Gilda and yanked her to the ground.

"Jarrah? Waseem Jarrah?"

"What are you doing?" Gilda said as her body folded underneath Jana's pull.

"You are probably wondering something pointless, Agent Baker, like how I obtained your cell phone number. And that leads you to what must be a very terrifying thought: whether or not I am also tracking your movements with it, or perhaps if I am watching you right now."

Jana's breathing rate went into overdrive.

"I have come into a great deal of wealth, Miss Baker, and can obtain a great many things. But it is *information* that I value most. Information is a most valuable commodity, don't you think?"

Jana leaned across Gilda, hoping to shield her from the rifle shot she feared was about to come, then began a frantic search inside her backpack for anything she could use as a weapon.

"I'm going to find you, Jarrah. And when I do—"

"You're going to what?" he interrupted. "Kill me? Well, after I successfully vaporized your CIA headquarters a few months ago with a nuclear weapon, I would think you would want to do more than just kill me. I would think you'd have more concern for predicting my *next* target. Maybe you should be protecting your FBI headquarters, or the White House? Perhaps I sold the warheads? Perhaps not. I cannot recall. Hmmm, where did I put those warheads?" he said through a grin Jana could feel across the phone. "But, I digress."

Jana began piecing together the thoughts streaming through her mind. *Where the hell is he? Is he watching me right now? I've got to think . . .*

He continued. "I spent many years in your country, Agent Baker." His tone deepened. "And I'm still trying to wipe the stench from my skin." Then he almost yelled, "The CIA, *the beast*, got what it deserved, and Allah was pleased." Jana heard him take a deep breath. "However, I didn't call to tell you to be careful and avoid twisting an ankle as you finish your hike. I called to tell you that *it's more personal this time.* In my previous attacks, I was unconcerned about who got in my way. But now I've taken a liking to you. You killed someone very dear to me, and I will ensure you feel the pain of your transgressions."

Gilda squirmed underneath Jana. "What is wrong with you? Get off of me!" But Jana leaned her weight on top to keep the woman shielded from the potential threat.

"Stay down, Gilda," Jana whispered. "Personal, you say?" she said into the phone. "Personal? Two years ago, you were the one that sent Shakey Kunde to detonate a nuclear weapon on US soil. What did you think I was going to do? Sit there and let him murder sixteen thousand innocent Americans? You sent him to die. He may as well have been dead before he entered that festival. And you blame *me* for his death? Our psychological profiles were right. You *are* insane."

"Watch your tone, Agent Baker," Jarrah belted. "You might be surprised at how inaccurate your little psychological profile is. I'll admit, I was focused on wiping the CIA from the face of the earth. But when my second nuclear device detonated, I felt a calm inside myself unlike anything I could have imagined. Destroying the CIA was the realization of a dream." Then the vinegar returned to his voice. "My path is set, Miss Baker. I have chosen my next target. Shortly you will witness the beginning of a game you and I are to play, a game of death, and the stakes have never been higher. Someone very important to you will die. You should consider their death to be a small atonement in the debt I intend to extract from you."

Oh my God. He's going to kill Cade.

"I do have one more thing to say to you, and it is this."

Jana could almost feel his smile again through the phone, but then his voice became stilted.

"*I heard one say in a voice like thunder, 'Come!'*"

To Jana, it sounded scripted, as if he was quoting something from memory or reading the words off a page.

"And you needn't bother trying to trace this call," he said. "I only use a cellphone once, then it gets destroyed. I am not stupid, you should know that by now. Say goodbye to your loved one, Agent Baker."

"What the hell does that mean? A voice like thunder? Come?" Jana paused. "Jarrah? Jarrah?" The call went dead. "Prick."

"Get off of me." Gilda squirmed. "You're crushing my ribs!"

"Sorry, Gilda. I thought he was here. I thought he was watching us."

"Who? Who's watching us?"

"I've got to call Cade." Jana's fingers shook as adrenaline surged into her veins. She navigated her list of contacts on the phone to find his information. "Dammit!" she yelled as she tapped on the wrong contact.

"Jana, you're scaring me! Here," Gilda said, "give me the phone. Who do you need to call?"

"Cade! I need to call Cade right now!"

"Okay, okay. Calm down. Here's his contact. It's dialing now." Jana yanked the phone back.

"I'm not hearing anything. It's not ringing. Come on, Cade. Pick up, pick up." But there was only silence. Jana looked at the phone. "The signal. It's down to one bar and even that keeps disappearing. The call isn't going through!"

"Well come on," Gilda said as she grabbed Jana's backpack and began to jog. "The town of Melide is just down the hill. We'll get a signal there. Now, tell me what's going on."

Jana squelched tears before they could form as the two friends ran downhill in the direction of the town.

2

TARGET ACQUIRED

Melide, Spain

By the time they reached the edge of town, a faint cell signal had emerged. Jana panted in exhaustion but wasted no time placing the call. This time, the phone rang.

"Come on, Cade. Pick up."

On the fourth ring, he answered.

"Well, if it isn't my—"

"Cade! Whatever you're doing, get to a safe place. Don't question me! Do it now!"

Gilda could see the terror in Jana's face and held her hand over her mouth.

"Jana," Cade said, "what are you talking about? I'm in a perfectly safe place. What's the matter?"

"Where are you? Tell me where you are!"

"I'm at The Box, NSA headquarters. I work here, remember? What's the matter? I'm in the operations center. Where did you think I was? Tell me what's going on."

"Don't leave the building, Cade. Stay at NSA. Do you understand me?"

"Babe, sure, I understand. But what's happening? Is this

another one of those top-secret things you're not supposed to tell me about? You know that my security clearance is higher than yours, right?"

The attempt at levity went nowhere as Jana's emotions overwhelmed her. She slumped to the ground and her throat locked tight. Gilda knelt beside her and put her arm around Jana.

"I thought . . . I thought I'd lost you."

"Why?"

"Jarrah! Jarrah is in the open. Somehow he got my cell number and I think he knows where I am. He called me, Cade. He said he was going to exact revenge on me for killing Skakey Kunde. He knows I'm on this hike and said he was going to kill someone close to me."

"Okay, now calm down. I'm fine, okay? Nobody can get to me in here. It's you I'm worried about. Where are you right now?"

"We're in a little hamlet called Melide. It's about—"

"It's four hundred and eighty miles from where your hike started, and twenty miles from where it ends, I know."

"How do you know that? Is NSA tracking me? Do you have a drone up there or something?"

"A drone, that's not a bad idea. Why didn't I think of that? No, of course I don't have a drone tracking you. A guy could get in trouble for tracking his girlfriend with a government-owned surveillance drone."

"Cade, my cell coverage sucks out here. You need to call this in. You need a security team around you. This is not a joke."

"I hardly think Jarrah is going to go to all the trouble to kill someone like me, Jana. It's too risky. Besides, Jarrah isn't into that. He masterminded the only nuclear attack that's ever happened on American soil. Killing someone like me isn't his style."

9

"You didn't hear his voice. And besides, he's a nutjob, remember? He's completely insane. I'm telling you, he's going to kill someone close to me. He sounded like he was going to do it immediately. If not you, who is he talking about? My parents died when I was a child. My grandparents are gone . . . and Jarrah wouldn't have called and given me much advanced notice. He would have waited until the last second, right before he did it, you know? Cade, if it's not you, then who? Jarrah is about to kill someone. We have to think!"

"It could be Kyle," Cade said. "But hold on, I think he's still here too."

"Still there? What do you mean? Kyle is FBI. He doesn't have an office inside The Box."

"Jana, you and your gorgeous blonde hair have been out of circulation for two months, traipsing your way across the Camino trail in Spain, remember? You've been away from *me* for two months, which I'm still mad at you about, by the way. Kyle is not FBI anymore. Not that it matters much. In the wake of the nuclear attack, the lines between what is FBI, CIA, and NSA are blurring. He's technically considered CIA now. He was appointed four weeks ago. Has his own team."

"CIA? Kyle hated those guys."

"No, he didn't," Cade said. "Once the majority of CIA's leadership was gone, killed in the blast, the power vacuum started. The whole organization is a shell of its former self. And, it's different. Kyle will be doing field work. He's a very focused individual, if you recall."

"All right, all right. Find him, right now. Make sure he's okay. And have Uncle Bill get on the line to Director Latent. We've got to get the full weight of the FBI on top of this thing—" But before the rest of the words could roll off her tongue, a thought hit her, freight train-style.

"Oh my God. I know who he's going to hit!"

3

AN OCCUPIED ROOFTOP

Across from the Jacob K. Javits Convention Center, Midtown Manhattan, New York

Rafael pulled a piece of plastic sheeting over his body and that of his weapon, a custom-tuned Middleton model 415SS crossbow. The weapon was capable of delivering a carbon-fiber crossbow bolt tipped with a razor-sharp 100-grain broadhead at over five hundred feet per second. The rain had slowed to a drizzle, and the last thing he wanted was to acquire his target through wet optics.

He'd never been tasked to carry out a hit using such a weapon, and had spent lots of time training with it. In the past, his typical weapon of choice was a Zastava sniper rifle. Zastavas are Serbian built, and he had used his favorite, chambered in 7.62x51 mm, to assassinate several dozen high-ranking officers in the war with Croatia.

When his new employer contracted him to carry out today's mission, very little had been said of his assigned target. At that time, all he'd been told was to proceed to the Northeastern United States and wait for further instructions. Before details were made clear, he'd even shipped the sniper rifle, which itself had made quite a journey. He had broken the rifle into parts and placed it inside a steel drum while he was still in Oman. The drum was one of about a thousand which were about to board a freighter bound for New York. When it reached the United States, the ship docked at the Columbia Street Waterfront, within sight of the Brooklyn Bridge.

Rafael had discarded the rifle scope that was originally attached to the Zastava, an old ZRAK ON-M76. He replaced it with something he was more comfortable with, a $2,700 Leupold model that had a much wider field of view and illuminated crosshairs. Once sighted in, the rifle had become capable of driving a tack into a target at five hundred meters.

But when his employer, Waseem Jarrah, had provided more details about the assignment, the instructions were very clear—the weapon for this particular hit was to be a crossbow. The instructions further stated that failure to use a crossbow would result in his not being paid. Thus, his archery training had begun.

Locating a suitable crossbow had not been difficult. He was able to locate it at a gun show in West Virginia and the purchase was untraceable. It would never have occurred to the man sitting behind the table that it would be used for any purpose other than hunting whitetail deer.

Rafael then took the crossbow to have it tuned. The archery specialist replaced the factory limbs on the weapon with those made of customized tungsten alloy. The man said it was the most powerful crossbow he'd ever constructed. Once the Leupold rifle scope was mounted, Rafael's ability to place an arrow into the center of his target became an act of simplicity.

The early afternoon sky was a dreadful mix of grays dappled with the black of the storm. The rain droned on, but sitting atop a building just across from the main entrance to New York's sprawling Jacob Javits Conference Center provided the perfect vantage point. His target would emerge, and once the one-hundred-grain broadhead bolt struck, the man would die before he hit the ground.

As time ticked by, Rafael became bored and his focus drifted. He raised the weapon and looked through the scope at an apartment building behind him and peered into the windows. In the darkness of the storm, Rafael could see into the brightly lit units. His eyes wandered from one apartment to the next, seeking out what pleased him. In a third floor unit, a young woman entered her front door and dropped a soft-sided leather brief case onto the couch, then made her way to the bedroom. "My, my, what do we have here?" he said to himself with a grin. His grin widened as the woman flipped off a raincoat and ran fingers through her long wet hair. "Oh, we are soaked, aren't we? Wouldn't we be more comfortable in dry clothes?" His laughter started low, but became almost maniacal as the woman pulled her black, skin-tight dress over her head and let it fall to the floor. "How very nice. Little black dress, black bra, black panties. Yes, well, I should think you would like me to visit. And how skinny we are. I do love a flat stomach." The woman reached behind herself and unhooked her bra, letting it, too, fall. Rafael's eyes flared at the sight of her bare breasts. She turned and disappeared into the bathroom. "Perhaps I should pay you a visit. Yes, I think a visit is in order. There will be time later, and we will get to know one another."

With the temporary distraction gone, Rafael turned his attention back to his assignment. Initially, he hadn't known who had hired him, and hadn't cared. The first payment had been transferred into his Cayman Island bank account and that was all that mattered. That and the fact that this job was the heaviest hit he'd ever been hired to carry out. This one would bring down a lot of heat. In the past, he'd hit high-priority targets, but this was on a whole new scale. The response to this assassination would be swift, and he could not falter in his escape.

He would leave no trace of his presence, with one exception: a piece of evidence he would deliberately leave behind. Once he had fired the weapon, he would have to move, and move quickly. His mind swirled with questions. *Why a crossbow? If silence is what is required, I could easily outfit my sniper rifle with a suppressor. And why deliberately leave this strange piece of evidence behind so that authorities would find it?* But questions such as these became mere afterthoughts. Even if he knew the answers, he would have accepted the assignment anyway. His line of work required one thing: complete loyalty to his employers. It was as simple as that.

A gust of wind pushed a wet blanket of rain in a sheetlike motion across the bustling Eleventh Avenue traffic below. He checked his watch. It would only be another minute or two before his quarry emerged from the glass double doors. Wind and rain would provide the perfect cover—it would be impossible for anyone to hear the muffled thumping of the crossbow as it discharged, much less determine the direction the shot came from. He would be off the rooftop and onto the streets below, mingling in the throngs of humanity, within moments.

He slipped further underneath the plastic tarp and brought the cold stock of the crossbow to his cheek. The view through the high-quality optics cut the dark rain and revealed a clear field of fire. He twisted the scope ring to zoom the view closer and began a slow series of exhales, preparing his body to make the shot.

Any moment and he'll be walking through that glass door. Any moment now . . .

His finger found the edge of the familiar trigger, and held.

The double doors of the convention center swung open and his target walked straight into the crosshairs.

4

REALIZATION

Melide, Spain

"Cade!" Jana screamed. "It's Latent. It's Director Latent. Don't you see? Jarrah is going to take out the director of the FBI. He knows Latent and I are close, and he'd view it as a way to hurt me and cripple the bureau. He already took out most of the CIA, and now he's after the organization that has thwarted him at every level!"

"Latent?" Cade said. "Oh my God."

"What? Do you know something? Where is he?"

"He was to be the keynote speaker today at the International Law Enforcement Trainers' Association convention. We talked last night."

Jana yanked at her hair.

"He's out in the open! You have to get Uncle Bill to call him right now."

"Way ahead of you," Cade said as his cellphone dropped from his hands.

He dashed out of his office and into the cavernous NSA operations center.

"Uncle Bill!" he yelled.

But Cade had no way of knowing that at that moment, Stephen Latent, followed by an entourage of FBI agents and media personnel, was pushing open a set of glass double doors that led from the Jacob Javits Convention Center and out onto Eleventh Avenue.

5

TO VANISH IN PLAIN SIGHT

Midtown Manhattan, New York

Rafael let out one long exhale then held it. He applied light tension to the trigger and the crossbow recoiled against his shoulder. His eyes never flinched. The full weight of the crossbow bolt, tipped with a one-hundred-grain Ramcat broadhead, rocketed across the street and entered the skull of FBI Director Stephen Latent just above the right eye. It tore a destructive path through the basal ganglia area of the brain and exited through the rear of the cerebrum. The resulting hole in Latent's skull was large enough to fit a grapefruit. The arrow continued on its destructive path until it struck a BBC cameraman just behind Latent. The bodies of both men crumpled onto the ground. Neither flinched; they were dead.

Rafael's motions following the shot were swift, but calm. He crouched behind the upper wall of the rooftop, disassembled the crossbow from the stock, and placed the weapon into a zip-up nylon carry case, which he slung onto his back.

From his pocket he removed a glass vial. The small ampule was filled with sulfuric acid, and contained a tiny, clear glass bead. He dumped the entire contents of the vial onto the spot where he crouched, and threw an olive-green poncho over himself. He was down the stairs and on the street in under ninety seconds. But he deviated from his well-rehearsed escape path which would have taken him down West Thirty-Seventh Street, one block left then one block right until finally descending the stairs leading to the Penn Station subway tunnel at Thirty-Fourth Street and Eighth Avenue. His plan was to be gone from the scene as though he had vaporized into thin air.

As it were, his particular tastes in women led him instead around the rear of the young woman's apartment building where he picked the lock on a side door, climbed three flights of stairs, then walked down the hall, counting units until he arrived at the fifth apartment from the left. Once inside, he found the young woman still in the shower.

No one heard her screams.

6

A NIGHTMARE WITH NO END

Melide, Spain

Jana pressed the phone to her ear. "Cade? Cade?" She leaned toward Gilda, who was still trying to catch her breath from the downhill run. "He must have put the phone down. Cade!" she again yelled, squinting into the brilliant Spanish sunlight.

The town of Melide had roots that could be traced to the tenth century. The main road was barely wide enough to fit a Smart Car. On one side sat an *albergue*, a type of hostel or hotel, and the other, a post office.

"Is this thing still connected?" Jana said. "Cade, what's happening?"

"Jana," Gilda said as she let her backpack flop to the ground. "Calm down. I'm sure he's working on it." She slumped to the cobblestone sidewalk to rest. Gilda's command of the English language was superb, yet her accent decried just a touch of Bavarian. "Stay calm. Do you have a good cell signal?"

"Yes, two bars. I can hear something in the background, but he's not answering me."

"It's not going to do you any good to lose your cool right now. You're doing everything you can." Gilda leaned against the post-office building, which shaded her face from the piercing sunlight. "God, I'm exhausted. You know we trekked twenty kilometers today?" Jana wasn't listening, but Gilda, never one to allow silence to fester for too long, continued. She let her eyes close and said, "He'll be back on the phone in a second, and you'll see. Your other friend, Latent? Is that his name? He'll be just fine."

"Gilda, you have no idea who we're dealing with. Waseem Jarrah is number one on Interpol's most wanted list. He is responsible for the nuclear bombing in America, and for a string of other terrorist attacks on the United States."

"Yeah?" Gilda said, exhaling. "You people sure do have a lot of enemies."

"Oh, and the Germans don't? Cade," she said again into the phone, "come on, pick up the phone."

A light breeze blew dust through the center of the tiny hamlet. A storekeeper across the way swept dirt onto the sidewalk.

"I'm telling you," Gilda said as she leaned her head back, "relax. He'll be right there."

"This is maddening!"

But Gilda shook her head and rested her eyes, her face again draped in afternoon sun.

Cade finally returned to the phone.

"Jana?"

"Cade! What's happening? Did you get Latent on the phone? Is he all right?"

For several seconds, all she could hear was Cade's breathing.

"Cade? Are you there? What's wrong?" Jana's eyes darted from one side of the street to the other. "Director Latent's all right, isn't he? Cade?"

Another gust of light wind funneled between the storefront

buildings.

"He's gone, Jana. He's been assassinated. In broad daylight. It's all over CNN. It just happened."

Jana slumped beside Gilda. "No. No, it can't be."

"They don't even know where the shot came from. He was definitely the target though."

Jana covered her mouth and she began to shake.

"We've got to get you out of there," Cade said. "Uncle Bill is on the horn right now with the Spanish intelligence service, the Centro Nacional de Inteligencia. Just stay put, they'll get to you."

"Cade, are you sure about Latent? I mean, are you sure it's him? What if it's someone who just looks like him, you know? He can't be dead."

"Jana, it's him. There's no mistake. He was coming out of the convention center, surrounded by news crews when it happened. The footage is all over the airwaves. Listen to me. You need to get inside somewhere. I don't like the idea of Jarrah calling your cellphone. You are in danger and I want you out of sight."

"He must know I'm on a hike, but I can't imagine he actually knows where I am," Jana said, wiping a newly formed tear. *He doesn't know where I am, right?* she thought. "I mean, think about it. It would be just his style. Call me and make me paranoid that he's watching me. His call to me was just a diversion. I think he likes to know his victims are squirming."

"Just get indoors. Do it for me, okay?"

"Cade," she sounded like a mom scolding a child, "I'm not in danger." She leaned against Gilda. "Besides, I'm not alone. I've got a friend. She'll look out for me."

Just then something slammed into Jana's right temple and everything in her vision went black. Her body flopped onto the street. The last thing she heard was the sound of Gilda screaming.

Across the phone line, Cade heard the muffled sounds, followed by a woman screaming, then the Middle Eastern voice of a man that spoke just one word. To Cade, the word sounded like "owe-woo," which, although he did not know, was an Urdu word meaning, 'come.'

Cade yelled into the phone, "Jana? Jana?" His cries were answered only by a muffled gurgling sound reminiscent of a person choking on their own blood.

"Jana!"

With the calmness of a dog waking from an afternoon of slumber, the man standing over Jana smiled, put away his weapon, and walked back into the hillsides.

Several minutes later, Jana began to regain consciousness. Her head throbbed. As she pushed herself upright, she startled as her hand landed in something wet.

"Oh, my head. Gilda? What happened? Why is everything wet? Did you spill your water bottle again?" she said.

But as she glanced at her palm, she found it covered in thick, dark blood.

"Gilda!"

Gilda's motionless, half-opened eyes glared back. She was dead; a single wound to the torso.

"Gilda, no!"

An hour had passed by the time the Guardia Civil arrived in the tiny hamlet of Melide. The murderer was nowhere to be seen. Two hikers who came into town off the Camino Trail later reported they had seen a man hike past them, headed in the opposite direction. They thought this odd, considering the majority of the Camino Trail's hikers walk toward the town of Santiago de Compostela, terminus of the trail, and not away from it.

As Jana listened to the hikers, she made eye contact with nothing. They described him as being of Middle Eastern descent, having narrow shoulders, and carrying a long, flat pack on his back. But when they described his hair as wavy and black, with a thick shock of white up one side, Jana looked up, and a cold shiver flashed across her body.

It was him. It was Waseem Jarrah.

Jana turned and stared down the narrow street, but her mind wandered into a spinning swirl and the edges of her eyesight became glassy. She saw flashes of Waseem Jarrah's face. But when another face appeared, a face she had seen in a thousand nightmares, her vision washed into whiteness and her hand began to tremble. A horrifying flashback from the events that had occurred two years prior played out in front of her as if she were living them again. It was all crystal clear. Waseem Jarrah's disciple, terrorist Shakey Kunde, pointed the Glock at her and Jana stared in abject terror as white flashes erupted from the muzzle. Kunde laughed a monstrous laugh and she felt the puncturing impacts of bullets slamming into her chest.

The next thing Jana saw was the shocking blue sky above the Spanish countryside as she fell back and her head slammed into the cobblestone street.

When she awakened a few hours later in a rural hospital, Jana knew she had suffered another post traumatic stress episode. The PTSD had resurfaced, and she had no control over it.

Her nightmare with Waseem Jarrah had begun again.

7

OF SWORDS AND DRAGONS

John F. Kennedy International Airport, Queens, New York

The flight from Madrid's Barajas International Airport to New York's Kennedy took just over eight hours. Jana followed the flow of passengers as they departed the plane and looked up only because everything in the terminal was so quiet. The airport was almost vacant. She could see just two ticket agents and a dozen men in business suits.

One approached her and held out a badge and credentials.

"Agent Baker, I'm Special Agent John Zucker, United States Secret Service. This way, please."

The other hulking men surrounded her on all sides.

"Secret Service? What's going on?"

"Homeland Security directive, ma'am. As of this moment you are under federal protection."

"Federal protection? *I'm a federal agent.* I don't need protection. You've got to be kidding me. Wait a minute, did you clear this entire terminal because of me? You can't do that. What about all the people that are going to miss their flights? I'm not in any danger. Don't you people get that? If Waseem Jarrah wanted me dead, believe me, I'd be dead right now. I'm perfectly safe. It's anyone around me who's in danger."

"Orders, ma'am."

"Yeah, yeah, orders. I know all about orders. All right, but don't get too comfortable in your new assignment. I'm not going to have a dozen sunglass-wearing linebackers flanking me everywhere I go."

"Yes, ma'am," the steely-eyed agent said before he spoke into a mic nestled underneath the cuff of his starched white dress shirt. "All units, all units. Sword is on the move."

"What did you just say? Sword? What is that, your code name for me? What does *that* mean?"

"Sorry, Agent Baker. We give code names for anyone under our protection."

"So what do I have to do with a sword?"

Zucker and the other agents surrounded Jana as they speed-walked from the gate. Their eyes darted back and forth so quickly they reminded Jana of coffee-shop baristas who had oversampled their product.

"The sword and the dragon," he replied.

"What?" Jana said as she struggled to keep pace.

"It goes back to meeting the dragon. If we face death in the line of duty, we consider that to be *meeting the dragon*. When you meet your dragon, you'll either cower to save your own skin or ram a sword down its throat."

"So how does that make me a sword?"

For the first time, he allowed himself to make direct eye contact.

"Two years ago in Kentucky, when you came face-to-face with the barrel of a gun and with a terrorist about to detonate, you didn't back down. That's what we call meeting the dragon and shoving a sword down its throat. You are the sword."

Jana quickened her pace. "Men," is all she said.

8

NEW TRAVEL PLANS

Blueberry Café, Avenue M at East Sixteenth Street, Brooklyn, New York

Rafael logged into the Gmail account. Here, he would find further instructions from his employer, if there were any. Instead of sending encrypted emails to one another and risking them being intercepted by the NSA, Rafael's employer had suggested a more simplistic approach.

Both Rafael and the employer had the login information to the account. When the employer wanted to communicate, he would compose an email, and then leave it in the draft folder. Since the email was never sent, there was nothing for the NSA to intercept. As long as no one found out this email account was being used by terrorists, the two could communicate at will. It was a low-tech solution, and it worked like a charm.

After successfully carrying out the assassination of the director of the FBI, Rafael found a single email in the draft folder.

This employer paid very well and, in all likelihood, the email contained instructions for another assignment. With his Cayman Islands bank account flush with cash, Rafael didn't really need the money. He needed the thrill.

He opened the email and read:

"A most successful venture. I congratulate you. Your timing was perfect. No doubt you were more than satisfied with the transfer made into your bank account. Based on the success of your first assignment, I have decided to continue your services. Your first mission was a target of the highest value, and thus, the highest pay. The next target, however, is of lower value and comes with lower pay. I am certain you will understand. However, the same bonus structure remains in place. If you carry out the assignment at the exact time of 2:16 p.m. EST, your pay doubles. And if you continue to be successful, you will receive new assignments. Attached is a photograph and details of your next objective. It is critical that you carry out this task at the exact time of day specified. Failure to carry out the task at the time specified will result in the termination of our relationship. For this assignment, you will use the vial labeled "number two." Remember, after you are sure your objective has been completed, empty the contents of the vial at the scene so they will be found."

The email contained a name, home and business address, cell phone number, and photograph of a soon-to-be-deceased target. He tore open a padded manila envelope that had previously been delivered, and withdrew vial number two. He held the vial to the light and stared at the contents. At the bottom sat a clear glass bead similar to the one he had left at the scene of the Stephen Latent assassination. It, too, was oblong in shape, yet no larger than a pea. Inside the bead was a tiny object embedded into the center of the glass.

Upon examination, Rafael found the object to be different from the one contained in vial number one. He shook his head, then pulled out his phone to begin searching for the next available flight to Louisiana.

9

TALES OF J. EDGAR

John F. Kennedy International Airport

"Agent Zucker," Jana said. "Can we slow down? I've got a headache from this lump on my head. My God, you Secret Service people walk fast enough to be running."

Zucker's eyes continued darting from one side of the airport terminal to the other as he and the other agents scanned for any irregularities.

"Zucker?" There was no response. "All right, all right, I'll let you do your job, as stupid as it may be."

The agent glanced at her from the corner of his eye.

"I didn't mean your job was stupid. I meant what I said earlier. There's no need to protect me. It's crazy. Waseem Jarrah does not want me dead. He wants me alive so he can watch me squirm as he attempts to carry out whatever he has planned. Believe me. I think I'm starting to get inside his head."

When she again received no response, Jana continued the one-sided conversation.

"Where are we going, anyway? Baggage claim is in the other direction." As the group continued speed-walking through the terminal, Jana looked through the massive wall of glass and out onto the tarmac. Bright, midday sun rolled through the windows like a sheet of glowing water. At the end of a gangway sat a Gulfstream 6 jet. Compared to the size of the neighboring Delta 737 and a Lufthansa Airbus A320, the corporate jet looked like a child's toy.

"We're not headed to baggage claim, Agent Baker," Zucker replied.

"Another flight? But I'm supposed to report to the New York field office. It's over that way," she said as she pointed toward the Manhattan skyline.

"Orders, ma'am." He extended an arm, leading Jana into the gangway to board the Gulfstream.

"Orders. When do I get to give some orders? And, hey, what about my luggage? I've got a backpack with all my stuff in it."

"Already on board the plane, ma'am. This way, please."

"Already on board? How did you get my luggage on the plane already?"

As Jana, Zucker, and the other Secret Service agents boarded the jet, the engines revved in preparation for departure. Jana took a seat and noticed all the window shades were closed.

"I've been on this plane before. This is Bureau. I was on it with Director Latent." She paused and thought about how Stephen Latent's body was probably on a cold slab at the coroner's office, and it gave her pause. Before her throat could tighten, she lifted the window shade to look at anything that might distract her.

Zucker lunged forward and yanked it down.

"Please don't do that. Security. I'll ask you to switch seats now, ma'am."

"Well, you boys are thorough, I must say." As Jana switched to another seat, the plane began to push back. "No, seriously. How is it that my luggage is already on board?"

33

Agent Zucker let out a long exhale, and the tension in his shoulders seemed to abate.

"I would think that you, being Bureau, would know that."

"What do you mean?"

"The stories about J. Edgar Hoover? When he was director of the FBI, and would visit a field office, two FBI agents from that office would be expected to drive him from the plane to his hotel. The roads in that town would be blocked off, like we do today for the president. And when Hoover arrived at his hotel, he expected his luggage to be in his room."

"Okay," she said, "so one of the agents driving him would grab the luggage out of the trunk and run them upstairs. It's an arrogant thing for him to require, but how hard is that?"

"You've never heard these stories, have you? He never allowed his luggage to be in the car with them as they sped through town. Two separate agents had to grab the luggage out of the plane and rush it to the hotel before he arrived. The problem being, Hoover would depart the airport first, and the second car of agents didn't have the benefit of driving through blocked-off roads."

"That's not just arrogant," Jana said as the plane accelerated down the runway, "that's pompous. Where are we going, anyway?"

"Fort Meade, Maryland, ma'am."

"NSA? Why are we going to The Box?"

"Homeland Security set up a joint task force there. It looks like Congress is going to merge all of us even further under one umbrella. Since CIA headquarters was destroyed, Fort Meade is shaping up to be the location of the new combined agency."

"Man, I *have* been out of circulation for a while. I go away for a couple of months and everything goes to hell."

10

A SCOUTING MISSION

Saint Tammany Parish, just north of New Orleans, Louisiana

The administration building of the Saint Tammany Parish Sheriff was larger than Rafael had pictured. The modern, two-story complex sported a tall, glass-lined lobby entrance with an adjoining jail. The outer walls of the jail itself were smooth cement which melded into the glass structure with ease. The property sat nestled among residential neighborhoods and was bordered by Louisiana Interstate 12, a six-laner that ran the northern border of Lake Pontchartrain, just north of New Orleans.

In the morning darkness, Rafael strapped a sharpened pair of tree-climbing spikes onto each foot. He then ascended the seventy-foot-tall pine tree by jamming the spike on one foot into the tree, then the other, the effect similar to climbing a ladder. The tree sat on the property of a local golf course, on the opposite side of I-12 from the sheriff's office.

Once he was at the highest point, Rafael could see only two obstacles that sat between his chosen firing position and the intended target. The first was the highway itself. The interstate was not very wide, but even at this time of morning was traveled by a large number of eighteen-wheel tractor trailers. Since he would be firing from ground level, a passing truck could obscure visibility of the target.

The other groundlevel obstruction was a twenty-foot-tall noise barrier wall that lined this stretch of highway.

From his perch near the top of the pine tree, Rafael considered the possibilities. The shot was only about one hundred meters, mere child's play in the world of a veteran sniper. But since his employer specifically demanded the assassination take place at precisely 2:16 p.m. EST, the stakes were higher. A kill shot delivered at exactly that time would result in a 100 percent pay bonus, a bonus Rafael intended to earn.

He had worked for several employers over the years, and in the two dozen hits he had successfully performed, never had such a request been made. The time requirement added a new level of complexity to the already dangerous task.

In the earlier assignment to assassinate FBI Director Stephen Latent, the distance to target was also minuscule compared to his skill level. And he had to admit that he had been lucky with the timing. Latent had been scheduled to finish his speech at 2:00 p.m. and was to head to another speaking engagement across town. That gave him just enough time to finish his speech and traverse the sprawling convention center. As it happened, he pushed the double doors open and walked into his death at exactly 2:16 p.m.

Here in Louisiana, and anywhere an assignment of this nature was to be carried out, the one thing of paramount importance to Rafael was his ability to evade the area after the hit. Since the Zastava M07 rifle would be fitted with a silencer, he had little fear of his location's being detected. And in the broad daylight, no one would notice the flash from the muzzle.

His previous surveillances of this area afforded him one particularly interesting piece of information. The target, Sheriff Will Chalmette, worked the afternoon shift. That afforded the sheriff the ability to speak with deputies finishing the morning shift, and, later, those on the graveyard shift as they came in to the office. The afternoon shift officially started at 1:00 p.m. central time, 2:00 p.m. eastern.

The sheriff began his day by arriving about thirty minutes early. Then, around 1:00 p.m., he would assemble his officers and give them an update. And just as officers prepared to go on patrol, Chalmette would do one thing of particular interest to Rafael. He would go outside and talk with officers as they pumped fuel into their squad cars.

The local parish could only afford to have a single gas pump at the station, so Sheriff Chalmette had ample opportunity to speak with several officers each day as they fueled up. It was during this time that Rafael had the best opportunity. His intention was to drop Will Chalmette into a pool of his own blood and brain matter at exactly 1:16 p.m. Central Time. Then he'd make his escape through the golf course onto adjoining neighborhood streets. Being separated from the sheriff's office by an interstate and a twenty-foot-tall sound barrier wall would make his escape all too easy.

Then the only hard part of this whole job began—the job of cutting a circular hole into the sound-barrier wall from which he would fire his weapon. Rafael descended the tree and began his preparations.

11

HOMECOMING

Headquarters of the National Security Agency, aka, 'The Box.' Fort Meade, Maryland.

As Jana walked into the vast operations center, she spotted Cade on the far side leaning over the desk of an analyst nicknamed "Knuckles," a kid so young his face barely produced peach fuzz. They had not seen each other since she began her trek across Spain two months prior, and she double-stepped toward him.

But as they went to embrace, she was pounced upon by her sixty-pound service dog, a caramel-colored Lab, Australian Shepherd mix. The force knocked her to the ground and she was greeted with a full face pasting.

"Coconut! My God, dog. Yes, yes, I'm glad to see you too," she laughed. "Man, that hurt. I know, I know, boy."

As Jana lay on her back, the dog stood atop her and continued licking her face.

"It's okay, boy. Oh, listen to him groan at me. He can't decide if he's glad to see me or mad that I went away for so long."

"Come on, boy," Cade said as he pulled the dog off. "Yes, it's okay, she's back. Let her up, you knucklehead."

Jana stood and hugged Cade.

"Man, you go away for a while and everything falls apart."

"Yeah, good to see you too," he said.

"I guess Coconut is mad because I didn't take him on the trail with me."

"I'm mad because you didn't take *me* on the trail with you."

"I'm sorry. I did miss you though."

"Yeah? Well Coconut was worried. He wanted to be there for you in case the PTSD flared up again."

Jana paused, knowing the Spanish secret service must have told US authorities about her being hospitalized, but chose to blow past it. "Oh, Coconut wanted to be there? Don't you mean *you* wanted to be there?"

A warm hand touched Jana's shoulder.

"Miss Baker." It was Uncle Bill. "It sure is good to see you."

"Bill! Oh, Bill. I'm so sorry about Director Latent. I know you and he go all the way back to Georgetown together."

Uncle Bill had aged in the time Jana had been gone. The toll of organizing a new, combined CIA-FBI-NSA, and the loss of his closest friend, Stephen Latent, had caused a deepening in the gray of his hair and cavernous beard.

His eyes found the floor.

Jana wanted to lighten the moment. "You still eat those bright orange peanut butter crackers, I see," she said as she picked a tiny orange crumb from Bill's beard.

"Losing Stevie was more than I thought I could bear. But when he died, you lost something very special, too. He was like a father to you."

"He was, but I still have you, Bill."

"Ha! I'm more like a *grand*father."

"Don't I know it."

"You look . . . different," Bill said as he stared into her eyes. "You look like something settled inside you. I'll tell you again what I told you before you took your leave of absence. Find who you are and what makes you sing, then chase it. And when you catch it, don't let it go."

He looked at Cade and drew a mental line between the young couple.

She looked at Cade and knew what Uncle Bill meant.

"I'll leave you two lovebirds to catch up. Go down to the commissary and get something to eat. But after that, let's talk about this phone call you got from the world's most wanted terrorist, shall we?"

12

RECOIL

2106 Margon Court, Slidell Golf and Country Club, Saint Tammany Parish

Rafael stood nude in the huge walk-in closet in front of a full length mirror, looked at the blood covering his hands, then began to laugh. At first his laughter was low and uncommitted. But as he found blood splattered across his face and torso, his laughter deepened until it was out of his control, almost maniacal. He fell to the floor and rolled onto his back as blood smeared onto the light-colored carpeting. After a few minutes, he stood and took a cursory glance at the expanse of the closet's contents. "You Americans have no dress sense," he said, shaking his head. He walked to the double vanity of the adjoining bathroom and rinsed his hands in the sink, then stepped into the shower. Once he had sufficiently washed the thick dark blood from his skin, he toweled dry and walked back into the closet and dressed in a pair of checkered slacks, a white golf shirt and Stetson hat, then looked back in the mirror. Rafael looked more like pro golfer Greg Norman than a sexual deviant hired to carry out another assassination.

He walked into the bedroom and smiled at the body of a once

41

beautiful young woman tied to the kingsize bed. "How nice it was to make your acquaintance. Perhaps we can do it again some time?" Blood covered the sheets and walls but Rafael took little notice of the mess.

He walked into the kitchen and removed a set of keys from a hook. "A change of vehicles is in order," he said. On the side of the key fob was a logo that read "Porsche." He walked into the garage, put a golf bag in the rear hatch of the car, then started the engine. He closed his eyes and listened as the engine roared. "So much more to my liking than that piece of shit I've been driving." Rafael left the vehicle he had arrived in and was on his way to his next assignment.

There weren't many golfers on the course in the sweltering 1:00 p.m. weekday heat as he made his way to the fairway of hole number eight with a golf bag over his shoulder. The hole was a 362-yard dogleg that ran along the sound-barrier wall bordering Interstate 12. With no one on the tee box behind him, he ambled off the fairway and into the trees through a thick area of briers until reaching the wall and the four-inch circular hole he had cut the previous day.

From the golf bag, he withdrew two separate rifle components and set them down. He then pulled out a short folding stool that flipped into place, affording him a stable base on which to sit when firing.

The weapon assembled, he positioned the golf bag just in front of the chair, about four feet from the hole in the wall. He leaned the rifle across the top of the golf bag and peered through the scope. Being positioned a few feet away from the wall would prevent the rifle barrel from being spotted by a passing motorist.

The view of the fueling station in front of the sheriff's office on the opposite side of the freeway was excellent. But the opening in the wall was narrow. It was like trying to peer through a length of pipe, then shoot through it.

Cars barreled down the highway, flanked by the occasional tractor trailer. Eighteen-wheel trucks provided a challenge Rafael knew he could not completely prevent. On his side of the wall there was no way to see one approaching.

In his current position, the line-of-fire was just high enough for the bullet to sail over the tops of passing cars. But if a tractor-trailer happened by at just the right moment, the bullet would slam into it. It was an unavoidable contingency, and the increased risk excited him.

He watched through the scope as deputies congregated around the fuel depot in front of the sheriff's office, preparing for their afternoon shifts. Then, from out of the glass doors of the administration building walked the sheriff.

Right on time. Rafael thought it odd that in Saint Tammany Parish the sheriff did not wear a uniform typical of a law enforcement professional. Instead, he looked more like an attorney headed to litigate a case. But it was him, all right.

Rafael steadied his breathing, then glanced at his watch. *1:15 p.m. One minute to go.*

In the heat and high humidity, beads of sweat eased onto his forehead as mosquitoes congregated around his face and neck, and buzzed in his ears. The sound reminded him of a band saw chewing through wood. It was a distraction, but one he had dealt with before. He lined up the scope's reticle on the forehead of the sheriff, a man who had no idea he was about to die. His breathing slowed further, which calmed the pounding of his heart.

At 1:16 p.m., the precise moment he was to carry out his assignment, his digital watch chimed once.

43

Rafael exhaled in one long breath and held it. During this forced pause, when his diaphragm and breathing muscles relaxed, he applied half a pound of pressure onto the rifle's trigger. When the silenced rifle discharged, it bolted into his shoulder. For a moment, his vision was obscured with the flash of the muzzle.

He looked in the direction of the sheriff, expecting to see him lying on the ground. Instead he and his deputies looked toward the highway as an eighteen-wheeler swerved into the guardrail, jack-knifed, then flipped on its side. Car tires screeched but the drivers could not avoid slamming into the overturned truck.

"*Mierda!*" Rafael said. He chambered another round, aimed and fired. This time the unsuspecting sheriff crumpled to the ground. Two deputies standing behind him stood in motionless horror as brain matter splattered their faces.

Rafael did not wait to find out if anyone had noticed where the shots had come from. Instead, he emptied the contents of vial number two onto the ground, packed the rifle into the golf bag, then walked through the trees onto the fairway.

To anyone on the course, he might have looked like a golfer who had perhaps lost his Titleist and gone into the woods to retrieve it. He waved to the foursome who now occupied the tee box on the eighth hole, and made his way to the adjacent parking lot.

It wasn't until he had driven through neighborhood streets, turned on Rue Rochelle Boulevard, then onto Interstate 12 before he realized his mistake. In the excitement of taking the second shot, he had inadvertently failed to collect the shell casing after he ejected it from the rifle. It was a costly error, but one he could not correct now.

13

CAUSE OF DEATH

Knuckles ran toward Uncle Bill.

"I've got some information about the . . ." But he stopped and looked across the room at Jana, then continued in a lower voice. "About the murder scene in Spain."

It was too late, Jana had overheard.

"You people need to quit trying to hide things from me." She was upset and Knuckles could tell.

"Sorry, Agent Baker."

"I told you a long time ago to call me Jana, Knuckles. It's okay. Just don't hide things from me. I'm a big girl."

"All right, son, so what's the big news?" Uncle Bill said.

"The Spanish secret service has determined the cause of death."

Cade, Jana, and Agent Kyle MacKerron looked at him, then at one another.

"What do you mean they determined the cause of death?" Jana asked. "It was plainly obvious she had been stabbed."

"Yes, ma'am. But stabbed with what is the question."

A scowl formed on Kyle's forehead. "What do you mean? She wasn't stabbed with a knife?"

Knuckles continued. "Not exactly, no. She was stabbed with a sword."

The statement hung in space for a moment. It was Cade who first spoke.

"A sword? You aren't serious."

"Very serious. The Spanish secret service confirmed it. She was stabbed through the heart with a broadsword."

"A broadsword. What? Is that a particular type of sword?" Kyle said.

Knuckles was in his element now, his head so full that at times, the knowledge had to spill out.

"Yes. It's a double-edged sword commonly used in the fourteenth and fifteenth centuries. In fact, the Spanish are saying that the sword even appears to have been an original. In other words, it wasn't a replica."

Jana stepped closer.

"You mean someone had an original sword from the fourteenth or fifteenth century? And they used it to kill Gilda? That's completely insane. Who would do that?"

But everyone knew the answer. The killer, from all accounts, was most certainly terrorist Waseem Jarrah.

Cade said, "Okay, look. This is all coming at us a little fast. I'm going to take Jana down to get something to eat. She just got off a nine-hour plane ride for God's sake."

As they walked away, Kyle said, "Watch out for the sausage pizza. I'm pretty sure it's been sitting on that buffet since yesterday."

Cade turned back. "Pizza? Kyle, it's nine in the morning."

"And?" After the couple was safely out of earshot, Kyle turned to Uncle Bill. "Bill? Got a minute?"

"Sure. What's up?" he said as he flicked a bright orange crumb off his short sleeved buttondown shirt.

"You know what's up."

"Yeah, I know. And I know what you're going to say about it. Jana's PTSD is back with a vengeance."

"You know I love Jana too, right? But Bill, we're not playing a game of Monopoly here." Kyle looked around the cavernous NSA Operations Center to make sure no one was nearby. "Lives are on the line. Her PTSD makes her a liability. If Jarrah has resurfaced, we're going to need all hands on deck, and we can't have one of them freeze up."

"You want her removed from active duty," Bill said as he crossed his arms.

"Jana is one of my best friends in the world. She's a better agent than I am. But I'm a field operative, Bill. If we get in a firefight, or God knows what else, she could black out, and that could cost lives. No offense, but you work at a place where no one gets shot."

"I hear what you're saying, Kyle," Bill said a little too loudly. He looked around, then lowered his voice. "And under normal circumstances, I'd agree with you. But this is different. This time Jarrah has put Jana in the middle of everything. It's my belief that he's going to call again, and every time he calls, we may learn something else."

"Allowing her to work this case is unsafe. You're putting people in danger, Bill."

"No, I'm not!" Bill again looked around himself. "Look, Kyle, of course there's an inherent risk here. But remember who you're talking to. I care about that girl as though she was my own blood. If anything happened to her, I don't think I'd ever forgive myself. But I'm also an NSA section chief. I have a responsibility to the United States and have been working terrorism cases since you were still in diapers. She might be a danger to herself or others, she might not."

"She may not make it out of this alive."

"If Jarrah has another nuke, none of us may make it out of this alive. But if he wanted her dead, he would have killed her in Spain. No, this is different. He wants to keep her alive so he can taunt her."

"Bill—" Kyle started.

"Your request to remove Agent Baker from the active list is denied."

14

JARRAH CALLS AGAIN

"It surprises me, Miss Baker," Jarrah laughed over the phone, "how far behind you are in the game, no?"

"This is not a game, Jarrah."

"Oh, is it not? But I am having such fun. My mood has never been lighter."

"You're speaking in riddles. In Spain, you said something about a voice and thunder and the command to come. What did you mean by that? What do you mean I'm behind in the game?"

"The most amusing thing is, with all your technology, you are unable to trace the source of my phone calls."

"Yes, hysterical. Now what did you mean?"

"Did you not go to church as a child, Miss Baker? Oh, come now. Surely your grandfather took you to church."

Jana's lips pursed. "Listen to me, you son of a bitch—"

"I certainly was not the son of a bitch. It wasn't *my* mother and father who abandoned me in childhood. Such cowards, they were."

"Shut up! They didn't abandon me. They died."

"Are you certain they just died? Is that what your grandfather

49

told you?"

"My grandfather was a great man. And how the hell do you know about my grandfather?"

"He was loving, kind, always honest with you? Is that it?" Jarrah was taunting her.

"I don't intend on discussing personal matters with you."

"And why not? He is dead, is he not? It's the question of your grandfather's honesty that troubles me."

"My grandfather never lied to me!"

"No? Are you sure? Your father was gone when you were, what? Two years old? And your mother when you were seven? You were so young. The memory plays tricks on us. How would one know? I suppose your grandfather told you your father died of cancer?"

"He did die of cancer!" Her mind scrambled as she fought to take control of the conversation and her own emotions. "I want to know what you meant when you said I was way behind in the game."

"You want no such thing. You are simply trying to divert my attention. You want to know more about your past. Did you never question your grandfather about how your parents died? Your grandfather was, after all, just a man. And your mother, his only child, had died in a car crash, a suspicious car crash. He was left to care for you. It's true, your grandmother was alive for a time, but that did not last, did it?"

"What makes you think you know so much about my childhood? You know nothing!" Jana choked her emotions down.

"You fail to answer my questions, Miss Baker. Have you never considered why they died?"

"What do you mean *why they died*. They died because they died. There's no explaining it. Cancer happens! Accidents happen!

People die."

He let a period of silence emphasize his next statement.

"Your parents abandoned you, and they did it in a most cowardly way."

Jana's blood turned to ice. "You know nothing of me and my past! My grandfather never lied to me."

"Well, perhaps the public records are wrong then."

"Public records? What public records? What the hell is wrong with you?"

"Now, let me see," Jarrah said, "what else is it you wanted to talk about?"

"Jarrah, what public records?"

"Ah, you are interested in our little game, is that it? Well, the game has begun and you are way behind. You are not the adversary I had hoped for."

"What public records?" Jana cleared her mind. "Jarrah, this is no game. Real people are dying. That nuclear device you set off killed eight hundred thousand innocent Americans."

His voice lashed through the phone. "And some not so innocent! I'm sure you have considered it from my viewpoint, have you not? When I destroyed your CIA headquarters, the beast itself, I liberated my soul and the soul of countless brothers in jihad. The beast has always been our sworn enemy. It is true that many 'innocents,' as you would call them, got in my way, but what's a few hundred thousand vaporized Americans between friends, right?"

"You are sick. You are insane, and I think you know it."

"You try to raise my anger, Agent Baker. This is folly. You are too far behind and will not be able to catch up. I, again, will win."

"What did you mean when you asked if my grandfather ever took me to church?"

51

"*Now* you are on the right track. Miss Baker. Are you not aware that the Koran and your Bible speak of similar things?"

"Of course," Jana said. "Both religions believe in the same God."

"It is deeper, Miss Baker. You'll have to dig much deeper to get to the bottom of this one."

"What are you saying?"

Jana heard a click on the phone line.

"Jarrah? Jarrah?"

15

SANDS OF THE HOURGLASS

NSA Command Center

No one on the team went home that night. Instead they bunked in temporary duty quarters, dormitories that were two floors below in the basement level of NSA headquarters.

The accommodations were spartan to say the least. Old college style bunk beds with metal frames and wire springs. Each room slept a maximum of eight people. It was relatively uncommon for the rooms to be occupied, but dorm spaces were available in times of crisis, and this was one.

Half of the hall was set aside for men, the other, women. Where that separation began, it ended in the communal bathrooms. Although each toilet and shower stall was well subdivided, the overall facility was shared.

When Jana awoke on the bunk, she found a blanket stretched over her. It was not something she remembered doing herself. And the thought occurred to her that perhaps Cade had come in during the night to cover her up.

As the stress and long hours of the terrorism investigation escalated, Cade and Jana had little time for each other. There was no time to talk alone. No time to eat together or catch a movie. No time for dancing, no surprise at the arrival of a bouquet of flowers. There was nothing.

She could see him though, daily. She would often find him looking at her from across the table or across the large NSA command center. They would smile and wink at one another but their relationship was suffering—another casualty of the war on terror.

FBI Director Stephen Latent had told Jana about his own failed marriage.

He may have been director of the FBI, a career goal he had obtained after decades of exemplary service, but destroying his personal life in the process was not something he had counted on. He divorced her the day he took office, at least that's how he had described his marriage. The extreme hours, the overwhelming stress, had all played a role in the destruction of the relationship, and he did not want to see Jana lose her personal life the way he had.

It was apparent he regretted every minute of it and Jana did not want to repeat his mistakes.

The relationship between Jana and Cade had started out in a most unlikely way. He had been the only material witness who could possibly help the FBI stop terrorist Waseem Jarrah in his first attempt to detonate. He just happened to be in the right place at the right time.

In fact, it was Jana's striking looks and soothing voice that convinced him to work undercover for the FBI in the first place. The two had spent a great deal of time working together, even to the point of acting like they were a couple on a date.

Prior to the case, Jana had dated only very attractive men. Not that that had ever gotten her anywhere. To her, Cade was something different. He was cute in a boyish way, but it was his innocence that captivated her.

It wasn't long before she could no longer distinguish between the role she was playing in the undercover investigation and her true feelings. The more intense their circumstances became, the stronger her feelings grew. By the time that first terrorism case ended, Jana knew her feelings for Cade were real.

Here was a guy who was genuine. She wasn't dating him for his looks or his money, she was dating him for him. For the first time in her life she had found something she didn't even know she was looking for.

And by the time the second terrorism investigation concluded, she and Cade had grown closer. It wasn't until they took a vacation together in Spain that she finally realized she was in love with him.

Jana's thoughts trailed off at the questions swirling in her mind. At the top of the list were Jarrah's comments about the death of her parents. She couldn't get them out of her mind. Had she been misled by her own mother? By her grandfather?

Now, in the bleakness of morning, in the sleep-deprived, pressure-filled third investigation, she didn't know if the relationship would survive. One thing she did know was that she still held strong feelings for Cade and those feelings were going unabated.

Her obsession to stop Waseem Jarrah was coming to a head. She was engrossed in stopping him, but she knew to do so might cost her everything. She couldn't allow Jarrah to continue. He had to be stopped, and stopped cold. And this time Jana could not allow anything or anyone to get in her way.

If she got the chance, she would kill him without hesitation. These thoughts played forward in her mind throughout each day. It was as if she understood her life could end at any moment and she would gladly trade it to shut the terrorist down once and for all.

Jana had grown up with her grandfather's advice, a piece of advice as simple and pure as the rays of the sun. He had told her, *Never do anything you're going to regret for the rest of your life.*

But that statement had an opposing side as well. She never wanted to look back with regret at *not* having done something either.

She crept down the hallway and peered into the first room. Kyle on one bunk, Knuckles on another. She tiptoed to the second room and found Cade alone, sleeping on the bottom bunk. She slipped inside and closed the door. It wasn't until she turned the lock that he stirred.

"Jana, is everything okay? What are you doing?" But she didn't say a word. Amber light burning around the edges of the door illuminated her sleek shape. Cade watched as she began to undress.

When the last article of clothing hit the floor, Cade could not avert his eyes. She was stunning, and he was just realizing how much he had missed her physical touch.

"Are you sure we should—"

But Jana put her finger on his lips and climbed into the bed.

16

THE SNIPER'S PERCH

NSA Dormitories, Fort Meade

Another day passed and the next morning came early. Jana awoke unsure whether she should scour the public records for information related to the deaths of her mother and father, or study similarities between the Bible and the Koran.

There was so little evidence to go on. At this point there were virtually no clues in the death of Stephen Latent. They hadn't even located where the sniper had been hiding. All they knew was that Jarrah was behind the assassination somehow. And it was certainly Jarrah who was responsible for the killing of Gilda, Jana's hiking friend.

Jana listened to a news podcast on her phone, the way she had done every morning, to catch up on what was happening in the world.

"WBS News at the top of the hour. I'm Mike Sladen. We bring you a breaking story out of Saint Tammany Parish, Louisiana. We go to our correspondent in the field, Charlie Rose, just north of New Orleans. Charlie what can you tell us?"

"Well, Mike, it's a gruesome scene. Just hours ago the sheriff of Saint Tammany Parish was murdered in an apparent sniper attack. Deputies who were with the sheriff say they were preparing for their shift when a major traffic accident occurred in front of them on Interstate 12. The accident involved a tractor-trailer that apparently swerved out of control and crashed. Several cars were involved. Then moments later, deputies report, the sheriff crumpled to the ground—struck by a bullet which was apparently fired from somewhere across the highway. Investigators say there is no way this was an accident. And in a strange twist to the story, Mike, it turns out the driver of the tractor-trailer was also hit with a sniper round. At this point the theory is that the assassin may have fired at the sheriff, but the tractor-trailer passed in front at just the wrong moment. The driver of the tractor-trailer is also deceased, and this normally quiet community is left wondering what happened, and why. Two sniper attacks have never occurred in the United States in such close proximity since the days of Lee Boyd Malvo and John Allen Muhammad, who perpetrated the Beltway sniper attacks in the Washington DC metropolitan area in October of 2002. In that case, the assassins used a sniper rifle to hold that city in terror over a three-week period. Even today, many label the two as homegrown terrorists, even though there was no link to any terror organization outside the United States. For now, this is Charlie Rose reporting live from Louisiana. Back to you, Mike."

"That was Charlie Rose reporting live from Louisiana, now on to other news . . ."

Jana pocketed her phone and tried to put herself together, then walked toward the command center.

"Where are Jana and Cade?" Uncle Bill said.

"I don't know where they are," Knuckles replied. "They're never late to anything."

Kyle glanced at the ground.

"You wouldn't be much for undercover work, Kyle." Uncle Bill said. "That look on your face tells me they are indisposed at the moment but will be here shortly?"

Kyle smiled.

As Bill walked off, Knuckles said, "What's up? Where are they?"

"Well, there was a coat hanger on Cade's door handle this morning."

The kid cocked his head to the side.

"Oh, I forgot. You're probably too young to have gone to college yet. How did you get this job anyway? Look, when you see a coat hanger hanging on someone's door handle in the dorms, it means don't knock."

Knuckles face flushed.

"Really, Knuckles, how did you get this job? I mean, not that you're not qualified. In fact, you are perfect for this job. But what are you, sixteen, seventeen? I can't imagine how someone your age could get employed by the NSA with no degree."

"Well, it kind of runs in the family, the NSA I mean. And besides, what makes you think just because I'm so young I don't have a college degree?" Knuckles walked closer. "Or a masters, or a dual PhD in physics and applied cryptography from Stanford University for that matter?"

"How did you get a PhD by the age of seventeen? That's impossible."

But when he saw Cade and Jana walk into the command center, he stopped, and a grin peeled across his face.

"What are you laughing at?" Knuckles said. "You don't believe me?"

"No dummy, take a look."

"So? It's Cade and Jana. What about them?"

Kyle thumped Knuckles on the shoulder. "Jana has misbuttoned her blouse and Cade's T-shirt is backwards."

The only thing that could distract Knuckles from the scene was the phone that rang on his desk. He picked it up.

"They found a what?" Knuckles said into the phone. "They said it was a glass bead? What the hell does a glass bead have to do with anything? Is the assassin making jewelry or something?"

He hung up the phone.

"What was that about?" Kyle said.

"Crime lab. The techs found a piece of evidence. They finally feel like they isolated the spot where the sniper was waiting when Director Latent came outside."

He looked up and saw Jana.

"Jana, I'm sorry."

"Dammit. You guys have to stop avoiding talking about Director Latent's assassination in front of me." She averted her gaze and her eyes found the floor. "You have to stop treating me like I'm a delicate child. He meant a lot to me. But that's why I have to find Jarrah and stop him. Latent would want it that way. He wouldn't want me to stop." She looked around the room. "There will be time for grieving after Jarrah is either in prison or dead by my hands."

"Jana," Cade said. "I don't like to hear that. You sound like a killer. That's not you; that's not who you are. And that's not us. We aren't here to kill people and you know it."

She said nothing.

Uncle Bill ran into the room. "What is it? You've got evidence from the scene? Show it to me, pull it up on screen three."

Knuckles threw his hands into the air.

"Uncle Bill, the data package hasn't even arrived yet. All I've got is a report that shows they found a piece of evidence right at the spot on the rooftop where they think the sniper crouched. It's a glass bead. But there's something weird about it."

"A glass bead? You mean weirder than the fact that it's a glass bead? Like what?"

"The homicide detective said the bead is abnormally shaped."

"How so?"

"He says it looks handmade. It's tiny, a lot smaller than a glass marble. He also says there's an object embedded inside the clear glass. I talked to him while he was examining it in the field, but he said he'll need a dissecting microscope to get the magnification he needs to see what it is."

"All right, people," Bill said, "let's get on the horn to the FBI agents on the scene. Tell them to get that glass bead to the lab immediately."

Kyle MacKerren leaned around the corner. "Already being handled. We've got several CIA agents on the scene as well. They, ah, just procured the glass marble and are examining it in a field laboratory at the moment."

"Good God," Jana said. "There are so many agencies on the scene, who's in charge?"

"The homicide detective is going to be pissed," Knuckles said. "Murder is their jurisdiction, even if it was the director of the Federal Bureau of Investigation who was killed."

"Jurisdiction-schmurisdiction," Kyle said. "He who has the most agents on scene has jurisdiction." He smiled. "Plus, all of us are practically working for the same agency now."

17

DEAD END

Bowling Brook Apartments, Laurel, Maryland

It became apparent that staying in the NSA dorms could not go on too long without a visit home. By the time Jana got back to her apartment, she was exhausted. With all the anxiety of losing Stephen Latent and her friend Gilda, the stress was beginning to pile up.

And weighing equally on her mind were the statements Waseem Jarrah had made to her. Jana wished she had been able to record those first phone calls. He said some strange things and she knew they meant something but had no idea what.

When Jarrah had finally stopped questioning her childhood, he had used the phrase "a voice like thunder," and the word "come." To her it had seemed as though he were either quoting something from memory or reading a script.

Between those cryptic statements and his taunting about her parents, Jana knew Jarrah was laughing at her. To him this was all a big joke, a game. He seemed like a person having the time of his life. With last year's successful nuclear attack on United States soil, Jarrah seemed to have achieved his life's ambition. He was not the same person anymore. Jarrah was right, his whole demeanor had changed.

Prior to the success of the nuclear attack, everyone had believed he was losing his mind. And Jana now realized the psychological profile the FBI had been building on him was completely worthless. His comments about her parents were particularly troubling. She remembered things from her childhood in bits and pieces. Memories of her father were mere flashes. He had died of cancer when she was just two years old. In particular, she had one memory of his standing outside the front window of their modest home in the mountains of North Carolina. She was inside on the couch, looking out the long span of windows, and he was throwing snowballs at the window to make her laugh.

She also recalled from somewhere around the age of six, her mother's admission that she and her father had never married. They had been in love and living together, but to Jana the knowledge had felt like a punch in the gut.

And then at the age of seven everything seemed to blur together. She remembered sitting in her second grade class on that terrible day when the school nurse had come for her. The nurse told Jana to collect her things and they walked to the front office. Once there she was startled to see a uniformed police officer. The only thing she could think of was that she was in trouble, although she had no idea why.

What the officer said to her was something she never forgot. Her mother had died in a car crash and her grandfather was on his way now. The shock was overwhelming. She didn't remember anything that was said after that, and her whole world came crashing down around her. There seemed to be no way out.

In the weeks that followed, Jana learned she would go to live with her grandparents on their farm in rural Tennessee. When her grandfather and grandmother arrived in their rusty pickup truck, she knew her life would be forever changed. Her parents were gone and they weren't coming back. About a week later the trio drove to her grandparents' farm and that's where she spent the rest of her youth.

Now, as an adult, Jarrah's statements began to make her question her own family. *Why have I never looked at the newspaper articles that surely would have been written about my mother's accident? Why did I never ask my grandfather about my father?* Jarrah's statements put everything she knew about them into doubt.

She heard the key turn in her apartment's front door and looked over as Cade walked in. Although they didn't live together, each had a key to the other's apartment.

"Hey," he said. "You okay? You don't look so good."

"Sorry. Just a lot going on right now, obviously."

"Listen, you've suffered a lot of loss in such a short time. And this case is killing all of us. No one would blame you if you took a few days off."

She glared at him. "A few days off? Cade, I just had a few *months* off. There's no way I'm going to miss a minute of this. I've got to be there. He killed Latent. I've got to track him down. I've got to be the one who catches that son of a bitch."

"I hear you. But it's starting to feel like last time. You always have this idea that it's you against him. There are a lot of us working together on this, remember?"

"I know," Jana said. "It's just that it's so personal this time. He's after *me*. And I don't mean he's trying to kill me. In fact, that's the last thing he wants to do. He wants to see me suffer, he wants to see me burn."

"We're worried about you. Worried about the PTSD returning. You've been doing so well over the past few months, but this is all so fresh, so stressful."

Lines etched into her forehead. "I'm not going to have another episode, got it? I've got control of it."

"Hey, I don't mean to upset you. But in Spain—"

"Screw Spain! I'm fine. But I feel like I'm walking around on plate glass. Everyone is watching me, especially Kyle, afraid I'm about to blow at any moment. I am not a little girl anymore, and it pisses me off."

This time it was Cade who had had enough.

"Hey, Kyle cares about you. He just doesn't want to see you get hurt, and he's worried. And you, you've always had this chip on your shoulder, like everyone around you is treating you unfairly. Sure, the FBI is a man's world, but there are few agents who have accomplished what you have. Everyone inside the bureau looks at you with respect. They don't treat you any differently, and it's starting to show that you are too sensitive about this male-female thing."

Jana crossed her arms. "I think you should leave," she said. It wasn't anger, but Cade could tell he had overstepped his bounds.

"Fine," he said, but turned before he left. "I care about you, Jana. I always have." The door closed behind him and Jana slumped into a chair at the table.

"Dammit," she said to herself. "The one thing Stephen Latent wanted me to do is realize that our relationships are more important than anything else. And I'm going to screw this up."

With a long exhale she reached down and grabbed her laptop. After all these years without questioning her childhood, she had to know. She had to find out what public records existed about the death of her parents.

In some ways, her lack of knowledge made her feel like a fool. Jarrah was playing with her, and she knew it. She thought to herself, *The SOB is probably laughing at me for questioning my own upbringing.* But even if Jarrah were playing mind games with her, she did have to admit she should have had more questions about her own childhood. But it never occurred to her that her grandfather would lie. He was such a gentle soul. And why would there be any reason for him to lie in the first place? Cancer happens. Car accidents happen. Jana could not understand what, if anything, there was to hide.

After ten minutes of scouring the Internet for search results, she finally landed on a single article about her mother. However, as was common for the day, the details of the car accident were not mentioned. Reading her mother's name in print brought those old emotions back, and they bubbled just beneath the surface.

But where her father's name was concerned, she could find nothing. Since he had died of cancer, the only thing she thought she might find was perhaps an obituary.

"I guess Google hasn't scanned every document and newspaper article from everywhere in the world just yet." His death occurred way before the Internet had spread into popular culture, so Jana knew that if any records were to be found, they would be in the form of newspaper clippings at the public library in her hometown in Tennessee. They may even be on microfiche, the old method of archiving newspapers onto a roll of film. But wherever the records were, it was going to take a lot more than a simple search to find them.

Exhausted, Jana closed the lid on the laptop, leaned her head onto the table and drifted into a fitful sleep.

18

SYMPTOMS

"It's here!," Knuckles yelled across the command center. "I've got the evidence package from the crime scene where Director Latent was murdered. The images from the rooftop, it's all here."

"Well, get it up on monitor six, son," Uncle Bill said as he clamored to make his way toward the monitor.

People from around the room got up from their cubes and congregated below the monitor which hung from the ceiling, surrounded by other monitors.

"Okay, it's coming up now. There are several shots. Here, let me get to the close-ups of the glass bead they found."

Cade asked, "They didn't find any other evidence?"

"No, nothing," Knuckles replied. "I just spoke with the NYPD homicide detective. He said the place was entirely devoid of forensic evidence of any kind. No cigarette butts where the killer would have been hiding, no fingerprints on the door that led onto the rooftop, no fibers, nothing. It was pouring down rain, so they figure any evidence would have washed away."

"What about video surveillance footage from security cameras inside the building?" Uncle Bill asked. "Did they catch anything?"

As Knuckles scrolled through the photographs of the rooftop, people scrutinized every detail of the scene. Everyone wanted to be the one to discover a clue that might lead them somewhere in the case, anywhere.

"Well," Knuckles said, "they have the subject on video, yes. But the homicide detective said it's a dead end. The sniper was completely hooded. He had on a backpack that apparently contained the weapon, but both he and the backpack are unidentifiable. You can't see his face, labels on clothing, nothing."

"Crap," Bill said. "Cade, Knuckles, I know the detective said he didn't see anything on that video, but I want you two to take a look yourselves. Make sure he didn't miss anything. Never hurts to put a couple of pairs of new eyes on it."

"Yes, sir," they chirped in unison.

"Okay, so those were the photos from the rooftop. Not much to see there. These next ones are close-ups of the tiny glass bead that was recovered."

Images of a small, oblong shaped glass bead appeared on the monitor. Each successive image zoomed closer to the object embedded in the center of the clear glass.

"And how about this glass bead?" Bill said. "Was there no forensic evidence on it? No fingerprints, fibers, or, I don't know, residue of cocaine, chocolate sauce, anything?"

"Nothing, sir," Knuckles replied. "They ran all kinds of tests on it. Nothing. In fact, the lab techs said they were a little surprised by that. They tested the outer surface of the glass for everything they could think of. And they said although the rain would have washed off a lot of evidence, usually something is left behind. They were baffled."

Jana and Kyle walked over.

"Can we zoom in tighter on the bead?" Jana said. "We need to see what's embedded inside the glass."

"Hold on," Knuckles said. "The next set of images are photos taken through a dissecting microscope."

"A microscope?" Kyle said. "Just how small of an object is in that glass?"

"No, Kyle," Cade said. "Don't you remember freshman year, your biology class? We're not talking about a typical microscope. A dissecting microscope is used when you either dissect something, or closely examine an insect or other object. It doesn't magnify to that level. It just lets you look really close, as if you're holding a hugely powerful magnifying glass in your hand."

"Teacher's pet," Kyle retorted.

"Men," Jana said. "So, what is that thing inside the glass? It looks like, it looks like a tiny horse, doesn't it? With something on its back, right? Am I imagining that?"

"Zoom up closer, son," Uncle Bill said. "I think she's right. Looks like a tiny person sitting on top of a horse. Damn that thing is small. And what's in the rider's hand?"

"I think it's a bow," Jana said. She immediately thought of Latent.

Knuckles advanced the images to get a view of the glass bead from all angles, at as high a magnification as possible. And sure enough, inside the glass bead was embedded a tiny figurine of a horse with a rider on its back. The rider carried a bow held high above his head.

Bill exhaled. "Well, that just about cracks the case. Anybody care to advance a theory?"

The room fell silent.

"Are we sure this was left by the killer?" Kyle asked. "Why would he leave this behind?"

"You're assuming it's a he, and that he left it behind on

purpose?" Cade said.

"Well, yes." Jana said. "First of all, it's one hell of a strange object to find on a rooftop, to find anywhere for that matter. And think about it. The glass bead has no trace evidence on it whatsoever. Don't you find that odd? If the bead had been there for a long while, say several weeks, it would at least have evidence of roofing tar, or something similar on it."

"I suppose you're right," Kyle said. "But if the assassin left this here, he left it for us to find."

"The question is," Jana said, "why would he leave it behind? Why not leave nothing so that we don't even have a starting point?"

"And," Knuckles added, "what does it symbolize? Surely he wouldn't have gone to all this trouble for nothing."

"You're right about that, Knuckles," Jana said. "He'd want us to find it, and he'd want us to find it for a reason. He'd want us to figure out what it might mean." She looked at Uncle Bill. "He's laughing at us. You know he is. He knows we're in here squirming, and he thinks it's hysterical."

"You bring up a good point, Jana," Bill said. "Let's add his personality into this. You've come to know him, the way he thinks. Jana, what is he thinking?"

Jana closed her eyes in concentration.

"Well," she replied, "we know it wasn't him who personally killed Latent. Jarrah was in the hillsides of Spain and murdered my friend Gilda at the time of Director Latent's assassination. That much, we're sure. So, he's hired someone else to work for him. He'd want to give us a clue to follow. Remember what Jarrah said? He said this was a game and we were way behind." Her eyes closed harder. "He was babbling on about something else. He said something about the word, 'come.' Like he was quoting something or reading it."

"And a voice like thunder," Knuckles said. "A voice like thunder. Anybody got any ideas? I'm drawing a blank on that one. You sure he's not losing his mind again?"

"No," Jana said. "In fact, I don't think he's losing his mind at all. I think for the first time in two or three years he feels on top of the world. He just pulled off what he would have considered to be his life's work—to detonate a nuclear device on US soil. No, he's thinking clearly. Which reminds me, I've been thinking that the psychological profile we've been building is complete crap."

"What are you talking about?" Cade demanded. "The guy has been a lunatic since the moment we first encountered him. Do you think he suddenly regained his sanity, if he ever had any in the first place?"

"Yes, I do. He's different now. He almost sounds, I don't know, relaxed. I wouldn't be surprised if what he told me on the phone, that quote he made, and the evidence we found, mean something."

Cade stood and squinted at her. "Are you sure you're not getting too close to this thing?" He regretted the words and the tone of his voice the moment he spoke them.

Uncle Bill scowled at the two of them. "All right, you two, what's going on? It's not my place to get into your personal business, but you two are starting to get at each others' throats and that compromises the mission. That goes for everyone here. I expect total professionalism in this room. Am I understood? We've got a terrorist situation to deal with."

"Yes, sir," came the resounding response.

"Cade, he's called me on the phone twice. He sounds like a person on a mission, a mission he's happy about. That's all I can tell you."

"All right, okay. It's just a little hard for me to swallow. And we don't seem to be getting anywhere. So we have this bizarre dialog from him where he's talking about a voice and thunder and the word 'come' and now we've got this stupid little glass bead with a tiny guy riding a horse in it. Are you telling me you think somehow these clues are related to one another? What do they mean?"

Jana sat. "I have no idea." She placed her head on the desk.

Knuckles started to pace the floor, mumbling to himself. Then his voice became more audible.

"A figurine of a tiny little horse with a rider on it. A horse with a rider on it, and the rider is carrying a bow? Does that just mean Jarrah had an assassin use a bow to kill with? No, it can't be that simple."

Knuckles paced back and forth and everyone followed his footsteps. He was lost in concentration. Uncle Bill watched him and smiled, knowing the boy was working.

"A voice like thunder. Who's got a voice like thunder? What is this, something to do with medieval gods? Or superheroes?"

"Superheroes?" Cade said. "I'm not picturing Jarrah, who grew up in the Middle East, as someone too wrapped up in Iron Man and Thor and all that."

Knuckles continued. "You're probably right. Well, I guess you'd have to be right about something, wouldn't you?"

Uncle Bill chuckled.

"Wait a minute," Knuckles said. "What about in the Koran? Is there something described where there's a voice like thunder? Anyone got a Koran?"

"Yeah," Kyle said. "I carry one with me at all times."

"Smart-ass," the boy said. "Hey, Jana? Oh crap, is she asleep?"

Uncle Bill stood and looked. "Leave her be. She's been through hell. And I'm getting concerned that she could be entering a state of depression. Victims of post-traumatic stress syndrome are certainly not immune to that."

Cade lowered his head. "I shouldn't have spoken to her like that. I'm starting to lose my temper awfully quickly. And she is too, to be honest. I think that time in Spain did her a lot of good. But when you put her back into a pit of terrorists, I think all of the stress comes crashing down."

Bill glanced at Kyle then back to Cade. "She's not made of steel, son," Uncle Bill said. "And you two don't exactly live normal lives, do you? We seem to go from one spate of terrorist attacks to another. Let's face it, we humans aren't built for this." Bill exhaled. "But someone's got to do it. Someone's got to stand in the gap." He spoke louder now. "I want everybody to listen up. This might seem like just a few sniper attacks. But this is just a buildup. This is how Jarrah works. He starts with a series of small attacks to disorient us, and then he tries to pull off something huge. We can't make any mistakes like we did last time. He got the best of us and shouldn't be underestimated."

Kyle put his hand on Cade's shoulder and spoke just low enough to not be heard by the others. "Bud, I'm worried about her. You spend more time with her than we do. Is she okay?"

"What's that supposed to mean?"

"Hey, don't get upset. I just want to make sure she's up to the call if anything bad goes down."

"Up to the call? Wait a minute," Cade said as he stood. "She might be suffering from PTSD, but I'm getting the feeling you don't think she should be here."

"Cade, we've been friends since undergrad. You've known me a long time. Have I ever done anything to break the trust between us?"

"No, of course not, but—"

"I'm trying to look at this objectively. So let me ask you a question. If the three of us walked out there and the shit went down with Jarrah, do you really think she'd be able to handle it?"

"Kyle, *I'm* not even able to handle it."

Kyle waited and finally Cade continued. "I don't know," he looked at Jana asleep on the desk. "I thought I knew, but I'm not sure anymore."

"Maybe Jana was right," Kyle said. "Maybe the three of us should leave all this behind and go down to the beach and set up a little tiki hut. We could sell suntan lotion."

Cade smirked. "That idea is sounding better and better all the time."

19

TREMBLING PSYCHE

Bowling Brook Apartments, Laurel, Maryland

In the morning, Jana startled herself awake and found she was in bed at her apartment. What was bizarre was that she could not remember how she got here the night before.

And then another realization came to her. It was the knowledge that her post-traumatic stress disorder had made an ugly return. *I'm losing track of things*, she thought. The notion turned her stomach.

It was then that she heard footsteps coming from the main area of the apartment.

Remind me again why I refused Secret Service protection?

The footsteps moved back and forth and Jana reached to her nightstand and pulled the 9 mm from its holster. She slid to the floor and crouched behind the bed.

The footsteps grew closer.

Fear impinged between her normal thought processes.

Jana's finger found the trigger guard, and a voice began to reverberate in her head. It was the voice of her shooting instructor from her trainee days at Quantico.

Double tap, center mass, then one to the head.

Her heart rate exploded. She pointed the weapon at the closed bedroom door, but as the smell of freshly brewed coffee wafted toward her, tension eased from her shoulders.

The door opened and Cade's eyes locked on the weapon.

She lowered it but thought, *Paranoia, another warning sign of PTSD.*

"Cade, dammit you scared the shit out of me."

"Good God, Jana. Put that thing away. Didn't you know it was me?"

"No, I don't even remember coming back to the apartment. How did I get here?"

"Kyle and I brought you. What? You mean you don't remember? The three of us drove from the office after you woke up."

"After I woke up? Woke up where? You mean I fell asleep at the office?"

"You don't remember putting your head down on the desk yesterday afternoon? We were right in the middle of a briefing and we looked over. You were asleep."

Memory loss. It's happening. Oh my God.

The blankness on her face signaled to Cade that she had no recollection of the events.

"Babe, this isn't good. Didn't the psychologist say something like this could happen?"

At first Jana ignored the question, but then thought better of it. "Yes, she said this was a possibility. But my PTSD was manifesting itself in those blackouts I was having, not this."

"Those blackouts you *were* having? What about Spain?"

She put her firearm away, and continued. "We're getting off topic. What did I miss while I was asleep yesterday?"

"Off topic? No, we're not getting off topic. We are talking about your PTSD. You're just trying to change the subject."

"I don't have time for PTSD! There's a nuclear weapon on the loose and I have to stop it."

"There you go again. You think it's just you against Jarrah." Cade shook his head. He was getting nowhere and he knew it. "We were talking about the glass bead and the potential symbolism. I'm worried about you, Jana. I had hoped your time in Spain would've helped you put the PTSD, the stress, the shooting, behind you. But if you continue to work at the bureau, I'm not sure it's ever going away."

Cade drew in a deep breath, then continued. "We're growing apart, Jana. You and I were doing so well. We were growing closer. We spent time together in Spain. But when you decided to take a leave of absence and go hike the trail, that's when things started to fall apart."

"Cade, I needed that time. I needed to go on that hike. The Camino Trail isn't just some place where I spent two months away from you. That trail has been helping people come to grips with the turmoil in their lives for over a thousand years. People come from all over the world to take that hike. It's a spiritual pilgrimage."

"I know, I know," he replied. "The Camino Trail means a lot of things to a lot of people. You told me. But you're still not addressing the problem. When the terrorism case went bad last year, and it turned out we were following the wrong suspect, it wasn't just a failure on *your* part, it was a failure on mine as well. And because of it, countless people died in a blast we should have been able to stop. And then we had to watch the news of all the devastation. Did you ever stop to think that I needed you during that time?"

"You needed me for sex."

"That's crap!" Cade yelled. "I can't believe you said that. Jana, this job is tearing you apart." He was almost yelling. "It's changing you. You are nothing like the girl I fell in love with." His face flushed. "I don't know you anymore. You have grown too accustomed to lying to yourself."

"Oh, and you don't lie?"

"No, not with you I don't. I tell you everything. But you, you hold it all inside, then you lie to me and tell me you're fine. You won't share anything with me."

"The difference is I lie for a reason." Wet heat spread across her face, but she was not about to let the building torrent of emotions get the best of her.

"You mean you lie for a living!" Cade said as a vein protruded from his forehead.

"You *know* what I do for a living. I'm a federal agent. You know I can't share everything with you."

"I don't expect you to share everything from your job with me. But you don't share *anything* with me. I want to know *you*, but you won't open up."

"I don't know what you're talking about." This time, her stomach clenched, a telltale sign that the emotional dam was about to break.

"Jana, I'm in love with you. Don't you understand that? I want to know you. I want to know the Jana that was still herself when we first met."

"I'm still her."

Cade put his arms on her shoulders. "Baby, you are not yourself anymore. This job of yours, chasing terrorists, it's changed you. My God, you don't even see it, do you?"

She folded her arms into his chest as he pulled her closer.

"I don't know what I see anymore."

"It's all the stress. It's you trying to be perfect. It's you trying to fit in with the boy's club of the FBI. And," he pushed her back to arm's length, "it's those three bullet-hole scars on your chest. That's what you see when you look in the mirror. You see those scars and you remember the flash of the muzzle, and you're not dealing with it."

Jana yanked free.

"Yes, dammit! That's what I see! Those scars are a gruesome reminder of the shooting, and I can't get away from them! Every day I see them in the mirror and I think back to it. I can't help it, Cade, I can't."

"Babe, I was with you when you went through the whole post-traumatic stress thing. But I thought you had worked through it. You saw the counselor for so long. But now, it's happening again." His lower lip trembled. "It's like watching a freight train come off the rails."

Jana's arms wrapped around her own torso and she slumped to her knees.

"No, no! Jana, don't drift off. Look at me." But her face washed pale and her shoulders began to shake. "Stay with me, baby. Stop it before it gets hold of you. Focus on me."

Her eyes drifted to his, and the grip of the impending post-traumatic-stress episode began to abate.

Her voice lowered to a whisper, and sounds came out in fits and starts. "How am I going to do this?"

"You're going to do this one day at a time. You and me, together."

She rocked back and forth, fighting the emotional forces tearing into her psyche.

"Why do you stay with me, Cade?"

"I love you, that's why. And I don't want to hear that crap. Look at me. You are the greatest thing that ever happened to me.

I was going nowhere when you found me."

"I didn't find you. Back then, I just convinced you to be a material witness in the largest terrorism investigation since 9/11."

"No, it's deeper than that. Before you walked into my life, I had no purpose. Didn't you know that? My life was just one of waking up and going to work. You gave me purpose."

"You make it sound so noble. Cade, *I used you.* I used you to break open the investigation. I used you to further my career."

The scowl on his forehead deepened.

"You used me? Is that what you think? Jana, you had no choice. It was your job to investigate that terrorism case. And it wasn't just to further your career. I happened to be the only person who had access to the encrypted files that my employer was trying to hide. Without those files, more Americans would have been killed in terror attacks. You didn't use me, you did your job. And you saved lives in the process."

A tear rolled down Jana's cheek, and she kissed him.

"You're too good to me."

20

A DISCOVERY

Bowling Brook Apartments, Laurel, Maryland

A ring tone indicating a text message startled both Cade and Jana as their phones rang simultaneously. Cade pulled his out of his pocket and looked.

"It's the office. Dammit, they must have something important. We're supposed to come back there right now."

"Jana grabbed a hair brush and ran it through her hair, then pulled it back into a ponytail.

"The bureau just doesn't give a girl time to get herself ready, now does it?"

"As we said before, these terrorists have no sense of timing."

Back at NSA headquarters, Cade and Jana walked into the situation room. Uncle Bill, Knuckles, and Kyle were gathered around a table, but no one sat.

Uncle Bill said, "Good, you got our message?"

Cade said, "Got your message? The blaring of the iPhones scared the hell out of both of us."

"Good."

Jana looked at the others. "So what's the news?"

Knuckles said, "We have some information about Director

Latent's assassination. It's a bit unsettling. Maybe you should have a seat, Miss Baker, I mean Jana."

"No sense sugarcoating it," Jana said. "Tell me."

Uncle Bill said, "It's about the autopsy, the autopsy of Stevie, Jana. We were just . . .we were just concerned talking about the details might upset you."

Jana swallowed. "What about it?"

Knuckles looked at Uncle Bill, who nodded. "Well, during the autopsy on the BBC reporter that was killed along with Director Latent, they removed the crossbow bolt from his chest."

Jana's stomach tightened. The thought of the BBC reporter and Stephen Latent lying on a mortuary slab with their chests cut open gave her chills.

Jana's legs became wobbly, and she slumped into a seat, then looked to see if anyone had noticed.

"What did they find that's so strange?"

"Well, obviously we wanted to know every detail about the bolt and the broadhead—the manufacturer, the type, style, composite materials, all of that basic stuff. We'll use that information to track down anyone who may have purchased such an item, the problem being of course that these are readily available. But we needed to see if any customizations have been made that might help us narrow our search."

Kyle crossed his arms. "Look, it's not as if we're talking about blood and guts here. Just tell her what we found," he said.

Knuckles exhaled. "They removed the arrow, then unscrewed the broadhead from the shaft. That's when they found it."

Jana's scowl deepened. "Found what?"

"Evidence. They found things embedded inside the broadhead. It appears that the base had been drilled out. That left a cavity inside where they found a strange residue."

Jana cringed.

"Poison?" Cade asked.

"No, that's what I would've thought as well," Knuckles said. "Instead it was packed with the pulp from a fruit. Fig, to be exact." He let that sink in for a moment. "We have no idea what it means."

21

PURPOSEFUL CLUES

NSA Command Center

"Fig?" Jana said. "What do you mean fig? You're telling me that the inside of the broadhead was hollowed out, and it was packed with fig preserves? That doesn't make any sense."

Uncle Bill looked over his glasses at her. "No kidding. And it's certainly not as if we are assuming the assassin spilled his Fig Newton cookies just before he fired the crossbow bolt at Stevie."

Cade looked at Knuckles with a grin on his face and said in his best British accent, "It's not a cookie mother, it's a *Newton*."

Knuckles looked like a lost puppy.

Cade added, "Oh, you're too young to remember that commercial."

"Commercial?" Knuckles said. "What commercial?"

"All right, boys, enough," Jana said. "Hysterical. Yes, the commercial where the little English boy gets in trouble for eating Fig Newtons in his bed. You two are a laugh a minute."

"Also stuffed inside the broadhead were two other things. An insect, a wasp, and a small stone."

"A wasp?" Jana said. "A wasp, a rock, and figs? Are you sure the lab isn't just messing with us?"

84

"Don't we wish," Knuckles said. "We had an entomologist at the Smithsonian's Museum of Natural History take a look at the wasp. She preliminarily identified the insect as either belonging to the genus *Blastophaga* or *Wiebesia*, which are very similar to one another. They're running more tests to be sure. The wasp is tiny, only about two millimeters long. We also had a geologist there take a look at the stone. It's a piece of rose granite."

"The question is, what on earth could any of it mean?" Uncle Bill said. "All we know at this point is that the crime lab has definitively confirmed fig pulp, rose granite, and a particular wasp. They're working to further analyze them to see if they can learn anything else."

"Like what?" Kyle said. "What Walmart they bought the Fig Newtons from?"

Uncle Bill said, "These are not Fig Newtons, people. These are just figs. You know, *figs*. It's a fruit. Jeez, it's getting hard to work around here."

"Oh Bill, they're just being boys," Jana said.

Bill continued. "They'll want to find out if the figs were fresh. Perhaps they can determine where they were grown based on soil contaminants, pesticide residue, nutrients in the soil, pollen grains, things like that. The same thing with the stone. They'll try to trace the origin of each item."

Kyle stepped forward. "I've got the FBI crime lab working double time on it. Who knows? Maybe it will lead us somewhere."

Cade turned to him. "Dude, you work for the CIA now. What are you doing calling the FBI's crime lab and making them work overtime?"

"I have people over there."

"You have people over there? Uh huh. What people?"

"Just people."

"You mean a girl. What kind of favors are you doing for her?"

"If you people don't get back to business," Uncle Bill said, "you'll go to bed without your suppers. Don't make me call Mrs. Uncle Bill Tarleton. She's not as forgiving as I am."

"Thank you, Bill," Jana said. "Let's think about the list of clues. We've got these items, the fact that Director Latent was killed with a crossbow is weird in and of itself, and a glass bead with a tiny figurine of a man riding a horse and carrying a bow. It's obvious that the figurine with the rider carrying a bow is symbolic of Director Latent being murdered with a bow, but what does that mean in the first place? What's a bow got to do with anything? And why is Jarrah going to all this trouble to leave these clues behind? What is he trying to tell us?"

Knuckles turned his head to the side. "Not what he's trying to tell *us*, what he's trying to tell you, Agent Baker. I mean Jana."

"Well I agree he's certainly trying to talk to me, I just don't know what he's saying. He said a lot of things to me on those phone calls. I just wish I had had a way to record them. I keep thinking back to his asking me if I'd never been to church. Do you think any of this has something to do with religion?"

"To a jihadist," Uncle Bill said, "everything has something to do with religion."

"And besides," Cade added, "this is a guy who grew up with Islam. I have no idea why he would make any references to a church, the Bible, Christianity, or anything like that. That is not his world."

Uncle Bill's fingers disappeared into his cavernous beard as he scratched his chin.

"Sounds like a wild-goose chase, the kind he would want us to go off on. He'd want us to disappear down a rabbit hole as we scoured the Bible or something."

Jana, however, was not so convinced. To her way of thinking, Jarrah was leaving clues purposely. Leaving clues for them to follow. Her concentration, however, was faltering. She was distracted by the comments Jarrah had made about her mother and father. The quick Internet search may have yielded nothing, but she had to find out. Then a wandering thought occurred to her and she stood. "Hey, did anybody listen to the news report about the sheriff who was assassinated a few days ago?"

Uncle Bill said, "Sheriff? What sheriff?"

"A sheriff somewhere in Louisiana. I didn't think anything of it when I heard it on the news. But he was apparently killed by a sniper as well. Witnesses didn't even know what happened until he collapsed. They never heard the shot, as if the rifle had been silenced."

"Two days ago? The day after Director Latent was killed?" Knuckles said.

"It's probably nothing. But look it up, son," Uncle Bill said. "What is the news reporting about it?"

"Yes, sir," Knuckles said as he spun his chair around toward his computer. "Hold on, let's see. Okay, AP Newswire reported that . . ." His finger traced across the monitor, "Looks like it was out of Saint Tammany Parrish, just north of New Orleans." Knuckles mumbled under his breath as he read forward, scanning for important details. "Just like Jana said, sniper rifle, didn't hear the shot . . . truck driver was killed as well. . . yeah, that's about it. His name was Sheriff Will Chalmette."

"What?" Jana said in a voice devoid of tone.

"The truck driver? Yeah, a truck driver was killed at the same time."

"No, his name," Jana said. "What was the sheriff's name?"

"His name? It says his name was Sheriff Will Chalmette."

Uncle Bill looked at Jana. "Is anything wrong, Jana?"

"It can't be. Is there a picture of him?"

"Sure," Knuckles said as he turned the monitor toward her.

She looked at the photo, then put her hands over her mouth. "That's Willy. Oh my God."

Uncle Bill said, "You recognize him?"

Jana shook her head. "I can't believe it. Will Chalmette? Are they sure?"

"Yes, ma'am," Knuckles said.

"He was a friend of the family, kind of an uncle-in-law. When I was a little girl, he'd come to the house every Christmas to see Mom. I called him Willy."

"He was your uncle?" Bill asked.

"Not a real uncle, no. When Mom was in high school, her parents took in an exchange student from France during her senior year. She became very close to the family. Her name was Michelle. That's where my middle name came from. She stayed in the US and got married to Willy. He was from Louisiana but I remember the two of them sitting around the Christmas tree, always talking to each other in French and laughing. I was little, so I don't remember much, but the two eventually divorced. Michelle, I think, moved back to France. He's really gone?"

"This can't be a coincidence," Kyle said.

Tears welled in Jana's eyes. "He always brought me marzipan. Dark-chocolate-covered marzipan."

"What?" Cade said.

"It's candy," Jana said. "Kind of a New Orleans thing . . ." Jana's voice trailed off. "I hadn't seen him in years." Her lower lip began to tremble and she turned away from them.

Bill looked at her. "Kyle is right, this is not random. Jarrah is behind this. He's chosen another person Jana knew, and we missed it. I want the three of you down there. We need to make sure they didn't find anything unusual at the scene where the sniper was crouched, like a glass bead."

"Wait, Bill," Cade said, "I get the fact that Jana knew the victim, but it's a longshot at best. He was a sheriff. Sheriffs have a lot of enemies. He was probably killed by some guy he sent to jail. Besides, if they'd found a glass bead, we'd know it by now."

"We need to make sure we see no connection between Director Latent's and Gilda's deaths, and the assassination of the sheriff."

"But the sheriff was killed with a sniper rifle," Cade said. "What's that got to do with—"

"Son," Bill said, "we just need to be sure. Yes, it's true it was a sniper rifle, but think about it. Director Latent was killed with a crossbow, and Gilda with a sword. Those are two seemingly unrelated weapons as well."

"Are you thinking we should expect more killings? With different kinds of weapons?" Cade said.

"Not just more killings," Jana said, "more clues." She stared off across the room. "To Jarrah, leaving a corpse behind is just a delivery vehicle for some new clue he wants us to find."

"Sir?" Cade said. "Louisiana? I'm not field personnel. I'm an analyst, remember?"

The smile on Uncle Bill's face widened just enough to be visible under his thick beard.

"That's what I told Steve Latent when he called and asked me to come pick up the encrypted data from you and Jana two years ago when this whole thing with Jarrah started. My wife is still pissed that her minivan was destroyed."

Jana said, "Didn't the government reimburse you for that?"

Bill looked at her over the tops of his glasses.

"You ever tried to write off the cost of your wife's minivan on a government E-06 expense form?"

22

LOSING FOCUS

NSA Command Center

With a new travel assignment about to commence, Jana became more aware of how exhausted she was. No matter how much she tried to sleep, she would wake but still feel tired. It was a never-ending spiral that she could not escape. It was time for a mental break from the search for terrorists.

She slumped into a chair and stared at the computer terminal through bloodshot eyes. Then a wandering thought occurred to her. She had been unable to find much information about her parents on the Internet. But she wondered if here at NSA headquarters, she could access her own personnel records on the FBI's database. Surely the NSA had access to all FBI personnel files. Perhaps there was more information there.

"Personnel records are sealed," she said just under her breath. "But these are *my* personnel files. I wonder if I can access them, or whether I'd get in trouble for trying. Like I've always said, take action now and ask for forgiveness later. I've earned the right to a few transgressions."

A few keystrokes later and she found herself staring at the FBI's personnel file for one *Jana Michelle Baker*. She laughed at the photo of herself: a head shot that reminded her of a criminal mugshot. In the photo she looked so young, so full of ambition, like it had been taken in another life. Now, three years into her career as a federal agent, she thought back to those days when things had been simpler. Perhaps Cade was right. Perhaps she *had* changed.

Much of the information in the file was info she was already familiar with. After all, she had submitted much of this on her original FBI job application. But what she had never seen were the comments made by various special agents who had interviewed her during that time. Here, too, she found few surprises. Most of it was standard reporting on her answers to questions during the panel-interview portion of the process—terse and to the point.

But when she got to form SF-86, the Questionnaire for National Security Positions, the preemployment background check, she leaned closer to the monitor. She read and reread the typewritten notes from the investigation. This, too, was all fairly standard. The FBI had sent agents to interview everyone in her past: friends, employers, school teachers, and the like.

After reading the comments from these people, she could see why personnel files were sealed. This was confidential information and she knew it. She shook her head and moved the cursor into position to close the file, but then a single name jumped off the page at her—a name she could not identify. It was the name *Richard Ames.*

"Who is Richard Ames?" Jana whispered.

The further she read, the more perplexing the notes became. Large sections of the document had been redacted—blacked out so they could not be read. Her only guess was that someone with much higher security clearance would be able to read the redacted information.

She scanned farther into the record but found most of it unintelligible. She could not locate any other mention of the name. Her curiosity spiked and she flipped back to page one of her employment application.

Her finger then traced across the monitor to the section labeled *Basic Information.* In this section was found the applicant's name, address, next of kin, prior addresses, and educational background. She had filled out this section herself and submitted it five years ago as she embarked on what had become a two-year hiring process.

And there again sat the name: *Richard Ames.* She couldn't avert her eyes from it. It was as if the surrounding information on the page became blurred in her vision. Only the name remained in focus.

It had a familiar ring to it, but she had no idea why. Her father's *first* name had been Richard. But *Ames?* What was the name Ames doing in her employment file? She didn't know anyone named Ames. Her eyes slid to the left of the document and read the label identifying what information was to be entered into that field in the first place. Her breathing became erratic. Jana closed her bloodshot eyes and rubbed them, then looked again.

This time her breathing stalled. She read and reread the label. It said: *Biological Father.* This form field was to contain the name of the applicant's biological father.

"Richard Ames? My biological father isn't someone named Richard Ames, it's Richard Baker. What the f—"

"Miss Baker?" Uncle Bill yelled from across the command center.

Jana bolted upright from her chair. She knew she was not supposed to read her own personnel file, and scrambled to close it.

"War room. We need to do a sitrep," he said.

Jana stood and walked, but her mind was focused on her personnel file.

23

LEAVE NO STONE UNTURNED

Fort Meade Flying Activity, Tipton Airport, Fort Meade, Maryland

In the morning the three friends waited on the tarmac as the Gulfstream 6 jet approached. A thin layer of mist covered everything, yet it was more humid than hot. It was early, and the sun had yet to crest the horizon in the eastern sky, yet light had begun its triumph over the darkness.

Cade yawned. "Can someone tell me why we have to go to Louisiana? This is a goose chase."

"What, you don't like Cajun food?" Kyle said with a grin.

"Love it. But that's a good question. Jana, I guess I don't even know whether you like Cajun food or not," Cade said. "In fact, the only seafood restaurant we've ever been to together is Casey's Crab, where we first got hooked on those fried scallops."

"No," she replied, "I love Cajun food."

Cade said, "I just don't understand why we have to go ourselves. Don't we have field personnel down there? I mean, it's Louisiana for God's sake. We're not talking about a foreign country."

"No one else knows about the clues we've been finding at these murder scenes. It's like Uncle Bill said, we've got to keep those details as close to the chest as possible for now. And even though the agents out of the New Orleans field office are aware of them, it's not as if they would have had reason to share any of this info with the sheriff's department of the murdered sheriff."

Cade said, "So what are we going to do? Are the three of us going to go out to the murder scene and the position where the sniper sat? I guess what I'm asking is, what is it that you people do all day when you're not in the office?"

Kyle shook his head. "We work, nimbleweed. We work. It's people like you who sit around in a cubicle all day."

"Oh, you're just jealous."

"Pencil pusher."

"Grunt."

Jana smacked both of them on the shoulder.

"Boys, enough."

"Okay okay, I get it. It's just that it would seem to me that crime-scene techs are better at evaluating a scene for stuff like this."

"From what Uncle Bill said," Kyle added, "the crime-scene techs found one shell casing from the sniper rifle. But they didn't find anything else. And they certainly didn't know to start peeling back the layers of leaves or pine straw, or whatever is on the ground there, to look for some microscopic glass bead."

"They didn't find a glass bead at the scene because it wasn't there," Cade said. "Seems like such a waste of time to send the three of us. Other than this distant connection that Jana has to the victim, I don't even see how this is related."

"Hey!" Jana snapped. "Willy was a great part of my childhood. With my father gone, it was like having a dad around. Christmas wouldn't have been Christmas without him."

"I'm sorry. I didn't—"

"I don't want to talk about it any more," Jana said.

"Listen, let's change the subject, okay?" Kyle said.

After a few minutes of awkward silence, Jana said, "It's a darn good thing that the government is sending a CIA agent and an NSA analyst. You two are not exactly the normal type of resources Uncle Sam would assign. But," she added, "it's good to be going into the field again." She considered her last statement for a moment. "Now that I think of it though, every time we are together in the field, all hell breaks loose. Kyle, did you pack your deodorant?"

"Funny, very funny."

The three boarded the now familiar jet and two hour and seven minutes later touched down in New Orleans.

Stepping off the plane was like stepping into a sauna. The brutal humidity mixed with the smell of rotting leaves was pure telltale New Orleans.

A uniformed sheriff's deputy stood leaning against a patrol car parked on the tarmac. His arms were crossed.

Jana extended her hand. "Jana Baker."

The deputy did a quick glance up and down her figure, then uttered, "Ah, Kenner. Virgil Kenner. Nice to make your acquaintance."

Cade noticed how the deputy was taken by Jana's physical appearance.

"You don't introduce yourself as Special Agent Baker?" Virgil said.

"No," Jana replied. "To me, when a fed uses the whole *special agent* title when meeting a member of local law enforcement, it always sounds kind of cocky. I'm really grateful that you are here to help us. This is Kyle MacKerron and Cade Williams. We work together."

"Well, folks, hop on in and I'll get us over to the sheriff's office."

As they drove, Jana said, "Deputy Kenner, I'm sorry about what happened to the sheriff. I mean that."

"Virgil, just call me Virgil. And thank you, ma'am. He was quite a man."

Jana wanted as much information as possible and knew that, in some communities, trust needs to be built first. It was something second nature to her.

"Tell me about him, Virgil."

"Well, ma'am, he was a real staple in this community. He's really done a lot to bring the deputies closer to one another, and even bring us in better communication with neighboring police departments. He was just such a great leader, and it pains me to think about him not being here anymore."

"Virgil," Jana said, "you may not believe this, but I knew him."

Virgil glanced at her, and his mouth opened slightly.

"When I was a little girl, he would come to the house. I have great memories of him. So, I think I know what you are going through. And, when FBI Director Stephen Latent was killed a couple days ago, it felt just like what you're describing. He meant a lot to me. He was there when I was just a green rookie, and he always looked out for me. I don't think it's hit me yet that he is gone. I'm just so focused on finding his killer."

Kyle started to ask a question but Cade put a hand on him and whispered, "Let her work."

"Thank you, ma'am. But, ma'am? Why is it that you all are here? The FBI already came up from New Orleans and asked us about the investigation. You don't think there is some connection between the deaths of Sheriff Chalmette and your FBI director, do you?"

"It doesn't seem like there is, no," Jana said. "But you know how they are—those pencil pushers just want to make sure they have a way to justify their jobs, so they sent us down here."

The deputy laughed. "Yes, ma'am, I know all about pencil pushers."

"Hey, not that we don't want to be neighborly, but do you think we could go straight to the suspected location of the sniper? I think that would be a great place to start."

Virgil replied, "Yes, ma'am. Whatever you say."

Fifteen minutes later Virgil pulled into the parking lot of the golf course that had been used in the assassination and pointed across the fairway into the woods.

"It was right down there. The number eight. This fairway abuts Interstate 12, and just across the highway is the sheriff's department. The shooter was down there."

"I hope you don't mind me asking some of these questions, Virgil. I don't mean to tear into fresh wounds. But, what do you think would make the shooter have known he would have a clear shot at Sheriff Chalmette from here? Why was the sheriff outside at that particular time?"

"That's one thing we all talked about. The sheriff had a habit of being outside at the same time every day. It's the change of shifts, you see? He was always involved with his men. Every one of us. He knew us. He knew what we were facing when we were on patrol, what arrest warrants we had to serve that day, even knew about most of our families. He was just that kind of man."

The group hustled across the fairway while a group of golfers waited on the tee box, watching in abject curiosity as the group disappeared into the woods.

"There it is," Virgil said as he pointed.

Before them stood the large cement wall that acted as a sound barrier between the highway and surrounding neighborhoods.

"See down there? That circular hole cut into the wall?

Apparently the shooter cut that so he would have a clear line of sight across the highway."

Jana, Kyle, and Cade ducked underneath the crime-scene tape.

"You sure you should be doing that?" Virgil asked. "It is a crime scene, you know?"

Jana turned to face him. "Virgil, I promise we won't mess up anything. But we really need to check this. Like we said, I doubt there is any correlation between this assassination and the others. We're just being thorough."

"Yes, ma'am."

"Virgil," Kyle said. "How much time would you say the crime-scene technicians spent over here?"

"Well, sir, let's see. They assigned me over here while the crime-scene techs were working. I was supposed to keep out any golfers or other people."

"You don't have to call me sir. It's Kyle, just Kyle."

"Yes, sir."

Kyle and Jana knelt down to scan the thick bedding of pine straw.

"Well I suppose the sniper would've set up just back here," Kyle said. "If he was back this far, he wouldn't have his rifle barrel sticking out the end of the wall. That's what they teach in sniper school."

"In sniper school?" Cade said. "Something all FBI agents learn?" He was throwing down the gauntlet and grinned.

"No, it's just that some of us paid attention when others were daydreaming."

"Daydreaming? As I recall, during undergrad, I was the one making dean's list, and you were the one talking with girls."

Jana interrupted the male banter.

"Virgil, does this little flag stuck in the ground represent where something was found?"

"Yes, ma'am. That's where they found the shell casing."

Kyle's experience with firearms sent him deeper into concentration as he tried to picture the scene as it unfolded.

"That makes sense. If he was set up right here, when he ejected the shell casing to chamber another round that's roughly where it would have landed, assuming he was using a bolt-action rifle. Now, if he was using a semiautomatic, that's a different story. The shell casing would've been much farther away."

"A virtual FBI crime lab technician in a box," Cade said.

"I'm not with the bureau anymore, nimbleweed."

"Not with the bureau?" Virgil said. "Not with the FBI? They told me all three of you were FBI agents."

"Don't pay them any attention, Virgil. They're just messing around," Jana said. "It's hard for them to keep a straight conversation going when they're together."

Cade studied the ground. "So if you were the killer and were going to purposely leave a piece of evidence, where would you put it? And something else that seems strange. Why was only one shell casing found? There were two shots fired. Where's the other?"

Jana said, "I've been wondering the same thing. I mean, if this was the same guy that killed Stephen Latent, we know he's going to leave that one piece of evidence for us to find. But why leave behind the shell casing?"

"Maybe he just forgot to collect it," Kyle said. "After all, snipers generally only consider one shot. That's typically all they get. But in this case, he fired the first round and it struck that truck driver instead. And as far as the second shell casing, that would have still been inside the weapon, which makes me believe that this was, indeed, a bolt-action rifle and not an automatic."

Jana nodded.

Kyle continued. "Sitting behind the wall, he wouldn't have had any way to see that truck coming. So he fires, but from his vantage point, nothing happens."

Jana jumped in. "Yeah until a truck starts swerving out of control."

"Well, yes, there's that. But the sniper would be hyperfocused on his target, and his target was still standing."

"That's right," Virgil said. "I was about twenty feet from the sheriff when it happened."

"Virgil," Jana's voice sounded as soft as silk. "I didn't know you were standing right there. That must've been awful."

"Yes, ma'am. That about sums it up. But you're right, sir. Truth be told, we didn't hear the first shot, or the second, for that matter. We just heard a muffled popping and then the truck swerved out of control and flipped over. After that, cars were screeching their tires and slamming into one another. It was a real mess. Couldn't have been more than a few seconds later, the sheriff is lying on the ground and blood is everywhere. A couple of the deputies behind him got splattered with . . ." Virgil couldn't continue.

"You were about to tell us about the crime-scene technicians. How long do you think they were here?"

"I'd say a few hours."

"And the only thing they found at this entire site was one shell casing. Is that right?"

"Yes, ma'am."

"What are you thinking?" Kyle said.

"I'm thinking that if the techs were here for a couple of hours, we're not going to find anything."

Cade said, "Just like I said. A dead end, right?"

A brightness popped in Jana's eyes and she turned to Virgil. "How much time did they spend on the other side of the wall?"

Virgil squinted at her. "Ma'am?"

"You said the techs spent a few hours working the crime scene. How much of that time did they spend on the other side of the wall?"

"The other side? Well, none, ma'am. The whole time the techs were working here. Why would they be on the other side, in between the wall and the freeway? I mean, we didn't exactly know which direction the shot came from at first, but once we found the hole cut in the wall and the shell casing, we knew he was crouched right here."

"Jana, what are you getting at?" Kyle said.

"Well, probably nothing. But I'm not going all the way home and then wondering about it later." She glanced at Cade. "I would regret that."

Cade nodded. "Regret is the poisoned soup of the weak. Regret is for suckers, for conformers, right?"

"Did you read that in a book or something?" Kyle said.

But it was Jana who replied. "No. It relates to never doing anything you're going to regret. It's something he and I heard from our parents growing up."

"The other side of the wall then?" Virgil said.

24

A NEW HOST

Center for Disease Control and Prevention, Arlen Specter Headquarters and Emergency Operations Center, Atlanta, Georgia

Rafael sat in the back of the van and squinted through a pair of ATN Night Vision Goggles. They cut through the darkness and illuminated his next target, Dr. Katherine Whelan, the director of the Center for Disease Control and Prevention. He then looked up at the ten-story building behind her, a tightly controlled government facility nestled into the sprawling campus of Emory University in Atlanta. It was silhouetted against the night sky and looked more like the corporate headquarters of a Wall Street darling than an arm of the federal government. But the property had tight security; of that, Rafael was sure. Years of threat assessments from the FBI and counterintelligence think tanks had seen to it that the facility had become a fortress. The CDC itself was spread across a campus that included several buildings. This one, the main headquarters, was the very definition of government overspend.

In addition to playing host for the CDC, Emory was also known as "the Ivy League of the South," and housed the state's most esteemed medical college and teaching hospital.

As Dr. Whelan walked across the secure parking lot, Rafael heard the familiar chirp of a BMW 5-series sedan being unlocked by her key fob. Rafael had memorized the car and every detail about it. It was a brand new 4-door, metallic black in color, and still had the price sticker affixed to the rear window.

He spoke out loud as if the doctor could hear him. "Your new BMW was a waste of money, Dr. Whelan. By tomorrow you will be dead, and my bank account will be flush with cash." He smirked. "It is too bad that you are a little old for my tastes, good doctor. And you have let your body become soft. Otherwise I would have loved to become better acquainted. Yes, not up to my standards. It is too bad for you, doctor. Most of the women I spend time with seem to enjoy my company greatly." Rafael thought about his assignment. "I do have to admit that I have no idea why he wants you dead, and in this particular way, but mine is not to question, mine is to kill. I'd love to pull this off inside your office, Katherine, but there are too many risks. No, I think your home will do nicely."

Dr. Whelan lived three miles away in the Candler Park area, and unlike the CDC offices, had no security cameras, no fence, no armed guards, no biometric scanners perched beside steel doors, and no barking dog. Only a basic home-security system stood between her and the outside world.

As director of the CDC, Dr. Whelan spent much of her time directing budgetary meetings, listening to threat assessments, and allocating resources to fight new biological contaminants. This day was not unlike many others. She had prepared a briefing for the president which would take place the following morning and had not left the office until 8:21 p.m.

When she turned down the twisting road of her suburban street, shrouded by oak and pine trees, it never occurred to her that this might be the last time she would make this trek home. Had she known her time on earth was numbered by hours, she would have set aside her steely exterior and thought about what her life had become, a stress-filled world of bureaucracy entangled in the warfare of modern medicine against man and nature.

In all likelihood she would have called her mother to say goodbye, her best friend Lillian to tell her how much she appreciated her over the years, and to apologize for not being there when her husband had fought cancer.

She would tell Lillian that she had been right all along. Life is not meant to be lived in a cubicle. Each day is meant to be spent reveling in the sun, and noticing things like the sound of rustling leaves on the trees, the simple smell of fresh-cut pine, and the glow of an afternoon's last light as the sun disappears below the horizon. And, most importantly, life is meant to be shared with loved ones.

But this was not to be. Dr. Whelan had no idea that moments after she stepped into the house, six freshly killed rats would be placed in the crawlspace underneath. The flea-infested rats were infected with bubonic plague. The fleas, the main transmitters of the disease, would soon detect the decrease in body temperature of the rat and seek out a new host.

25

TO COVER ONE'S TRACKS

Saint Tammany Parish, along the edge of Interstate 12

When they finally got out of the patrol car on the other side of the wall, the afternoon Louisiana sun was blazing. Jana could feel the heat on her back, and the humidity made it hard to breathe.

"There's the hole in the wall," Virgil said.

Jana again asked, "Are you sure the crime lab technicians never examined this side of the wall?"

"Yes, ma'am. Absolutely."

Kyle said, "We should approach slowly. We don't want to step on any evidence."

"There's not going to be any," Cade said.

"Leave it alone, Cade," Jana said.

A tractor-trailer rumbled by and the vibrations under their feet were only paralleled by the blast of wind that accompanied it.

"Kyle," Jana said, "look at that."

"Look at what?"

"Over there, right underneath the hole in the wall. How come all the grass is green except for that one spot?"

"And look at the wall itself, down at the base," Kyle said. "It looks stained or something."

Jana walked closer to the wall but stayed to the side. She leaned forward, wanting to avoid destroying any evidence underneath her feet.

"That looks . . . burned. Well, not burned exactly."

Cade said, "Looks like something burned by acid."

"Even the wall," Jana replied. "Look at the cement. Something dripped down and etched the cement. What would cause that?"

But it was only a moment later when it caught her eye. A tiny glint just at the base of the burned grass. Jana looked at Cade. "Not going to find any. Is that what you said?" She looked toward Virgil. "Virge, I think we're going to need that crime-scene team to get back out here. We may have something."

An hour later, one lane of traffic had been blocked off and the roadside swarmed with official vehicles. FBI vans filled with crime-scene technicians had driven in from New Orleans. The local crime-scene techs were also on scene but had been not-so-politely told to stay out.

The FBI had a long-standing reputation of treating local law officials poorly, then taking credit for solving a case. It was a reputation Jana would take no part in. So when she overheard the FBI's crime tech supervisor speak rudely to the acting sheriff, it sickened her.

She yanked the shoulder of the supervisor and spun him around. "Look," she pointed over to the sheriff's deputies and local crime-scene techs. "Those people are to be treated with respect. Three days ago they lost their senior-most in command. He was a highly respected member of law enforcement. You may *think* we have jurisdiction, but that's only because there are more of us than there are of them. If they want to get nasty, the attorney general of Louisiana will show up and hand your ass to you in a paper bag. Murder is a state crime, not a federal one. We are here by invitation, is that clear?"

The man glared down from his six-foot-three-inch frame, sizing her up. "I don't take orders from you."

"You do today!" With that she snatched his ID card from the chain hanging around his neck and studied it. "Out here, I'm in command," she barked. "This is my investigation and my responsibility. As far as you know, I might as well be a supervisory special agent in charge. You got that?" She dropped the ID on the grass at his feet and walked away.

"Jana, what was that all about?" Cade said. "You're losing your temper. I've never seen you like this."

"I know, I know. But that kind of crap pisses me off. To these people, they lost the same thing as we did with Director Latent, and I won't have them treated like that. This sweltering heat isn't helping anything either."

Kyle shook his head. "Man, I hope I'm not around when you really get pissed off. I hate to say it, but you need to get a hold on that temper. Carrying a firearm and having a hair-trigger temper don't go well together. No pun intended."

"Very funny."

A crime-scene technician dressed in a white fiber-proof jumpsuit and face mask yelled out, "I've got something strange over here. It's some kind of a small bead, but everything is covered in acid."

Jana, Cade, and Kyle walked to the edge of the crime-scene tape. Jana said, "Acid?"

He replied, "It's just like I said. There's a glass bead down there, but there's acid all over it. The acid is what caused these scorch marks on the wall, and burned the grass."

Cade looked at Kyle. "Why would you cover a glass bead with

acid?"

"I have no idea. But I can think of someone who might."

Jana asked, "Yeah, you going to call our hazmat guys? Agents Fry and Keller? Weren't they the guys we've worked with a couple times before?"

"The very ones. They specialize in crime scenes that involve nuclear contamination, but they're both hazmat trained. If anyone knows the answer to this, it would be them."

Kyle wasted no time in calling FBI headquarters in Washington and getting the two agents on the phone.

"Put them on speaker," Jana said.

Kyle described the situation at the crime scene to them.

"So the question is, if you were a criminal and wanted to leave a piece of evidence at a crime scene on purpose, why would you cover it with acid?"

It was agent Keller who responded. "Well, it would be a brilliant way to cover up any trace evidence. I can't say that I've ever heard of a case with this actually happening, but, then again, criminals almost never leave behind evidence on purpose."

Jana said to Kyle, "But the glass bead recovered from the scene of Director Latent's assassination wasn't covered with acid. This doesn't make sense."

"Well," Keller said, "it was raining that night. Given enough time and rainwater, the acid could've easily been washed free. But now that we know what to look for, it might be possible for the lab to pick up a trace of it on the rooftop."

"Wait a minute," Cade said. "Maybe that's why the lab said there was no trace evidence found on the glass bead at Director Latent's assassination. Maybe it was covered with acid as well, but the rain washed all of that free, making it nearly impossible to tell."

"Starting to see the connection now?" Jana rubbed.

Agent Fry piped up. "I've looked at the lab reports. I think you are right. We never expect to find a piece of evidence like that at the crime scene and yet find absolutely no trace evidence on it. That would be consistent with the glass bead at Latent's crime scene having been doused with acid as well."

Jana yelled back to the crime-scene tech who was now removing the glass bead with a pair of metal tongs.

"Can you tell what kind of acid is present?"

Without looking up he replied, "Portable chromatograph preliminarily identifies it as *sulfuric*. Sulfuric acid. But it'll have to go back to the lab to confirm."

Fry and Keller overheard the response. "Well, if it is sulfuric acid, there certainly would be no trace evidence left on the glass bead. In fact, it won't do us any good to try and track down the manufacturer of the sulfuric acid itself either. Sulfuric acid is sulfuric acid, there isn't any difference between one production facility and another. All contaminants introduced at the facility would be burned up in the acid."

"And," Agent Keller added, "from what I've read about the lab reports on the glass bead found, the bead was certainly homemade. Not something that can be traced to a manufacturer. In fact, both glass beads were. It's a hell of a way to cover up any evidence of where the glass beads were made."

"What do you mean, *both* glass beads?" Jana said. "Until this moment, we only had the one glass bead found at Director Latent's assassination. How would you know that this one was homemade as well? We haven't even seen it yet."

"The first one was at Director Latent's site. The second was just pulled out of the body of the victim in Spain. Apparently, the killer stuffed it inside her open wound after he stabbed her with a sword. That makes three glass beads. I am sorry, Agent Baker."

Cade put his hand on her shoulder.

"I'm sorry about Gilda, Jana."

But Jana's face hardened. "I'm going to kill that son of a bitch myself. And something else, it's time we go have a talk with the coroner here."

"The coroner?" Cade said. "You mean bodies on a slab and stuff? Oh great, that will be another first for me."

Kyle said, "And what do we want to talk to him about?"

"You're assuming it's a him," Jana said.

"My, my. We are sensitive, aren't we?"

"You have no idea."

26

A NEW DIRECTION

Monterrey, California

Rafael pulled into the side entrance of The Bayhouse Lodge and parked against the one-story building. The hotel sat within view of the Monterrey Bay, a touristy stretch of California's Pacific coastline. The area, adored by visitors as the place that inspired the novelist John Steinbeck, is also home to several military installations including the Defense Language Institute.

But it wasn't the history, presence of military activity, or the hotel itself that Rafael was interested in. It was the public Wi-Fi connection spilling through the walls of the aging hotel. If Rafael was to stay below the NSA's radar, he had to blend in with the masses, and accessing the Internet undetected was critical. To accomplish this, his method was to hide in plain sight.

The process was simple. Pull a car close to most any midpriced hotel, and an Internet connection was available for the taking. No hotspot login, no password, and no questions.

Rafael watched as hotel guests made their way around the back of the hotel, past the pool, and toward a large barbecue pit. The hickory smoke wafting from the fire reminded him how hungry he was. He laughed as he thought about what it would be like to witness the reactions of these vacationers as they were being told another nuclear device had detonated within US borders. But when his eyes landed on a well-tanned young brunette sunning herself at the pool, his focus sharpened. He picked up a pair of binoculars and watched as a man lying beside her sat up, said a few words, then walked toward the barbeque pit. Rafael's eyes traced the curves of her trim form.

He booted the laptop and after logging in to the Gmail account, found a new message from Jarrah waiting in the draft folder.

After reading the brief message, he closed the laptop and stared ahead. A fresh coat of beige paint on the aging hotel's plank siding shined back at him. His eyes then wandered back to the pool.

The message from Jarrah detailed the next assignment—one that would prove most challenging. "This assignment will not be easy. But there is plenty of time," he said.

The young woman picked up a towel and walked toward the hotel. "Yes, plenty of time. But whatever am I to do? Well, perhaps I can think of something." His grin widened as he got out of the car and followed the woman's path into the back side of the hotel, and down the hallway. Once there, he pretended to be distracted, as though he was searching his pockets for his hotel room keycard. As she unlocked her door, he grabbed her from behind, his hand stifled her screams, and he pushed her into the room.

When he was done, Rafael walked outside, backed his car out and took Route 1 toward Highway 68 as though he didn't have a care in the world. When he reached the town of Salinas, California, the birthplace of John Steinbeck, he turned south on Highway 101.

The Internet access had proved most valuable. And now that

he understood his new assignment, he knew why Jarrah had sent him to Monterrey Bay.

In the message, Jarrah described Rafael's new mission as one that would take place in two stages. In the first, Rafael would be required to procure the necessary equipment. To do so, he would wait until late at night, then break into the storage areas of a chemical-manufacturing plant owned by Hayland Industries. The plant sat just six miles away from his current location on Highway 101.

According to intelligence provided by Jarrah, the chemical manufacturer had recently been involved in a top-secret government project; one conducted at the behest of the Central Intelligence Agency.

The second stage of the mission would prove far more dangerous and Rafael began a series of mental exercises; he was running through all possible scenarios. To him, this would be the most exhilarating assignment he had ever undertaken. The risks and danger were overwhelming, yet the reward . . .

With Rafael's Cayman Islands bank account again flush with cash, and his sexual appetite quieted, his thoughts recentered on one thing: serving his employer, and serving him well.

27

HIDDEN

Office of the Coroner, Saint Tammany Parish

As the three friends walked into the coroner's office, Jana turned and jabbed Kyle in the stomach.

"Ouch, what was that for?"

"I told you not to assume it was a man," she said as she pointed to a sign on the wall. The sign read,

St. Tammany Parish
Office of the Coroner
Rosa M. Canray, MD

"Okay, you were right. It's a woman. You know when I said "him," I wasn't trying to be a bigoted, racist, segregationist womanizer, right?"

"Hey," Cade said to Jana, "remind me not to piss you off any more than I already have, okay?"

"Just trying to keep you boys in line."

Kyle said, "You think all this superhero FBI-agent stuff is going to her head?"

"I'm not going to touch that one," Cade said.

"What, are you scared? She doesn't hit that hard," Kyle said.

Jana grinned as they open the door. "I didn't hit that hard

because I didn't want to dent your delicate sensibilities, Kyle."

"Who told you I had delicate sensibilities?"

"I did," Cade said.

Jana flashed her credentials to the receptionist.

"We would like to see Dr. Canray, if she has a few moments."

The receptionist did a double take at the credentials.

"Yes, one moment." A minute later she was back. "Yes, you can go through that door, she's in the middle of an autopsy, but you are welcome to speak with her."

"Autopsy?" Cade said. "I'm not going into any autopsy."

"Oh come on," Kyle said. "You big baby."

"Yeah," Jana said. "You think we enjoy this? Come on, it comes with the territory."

Cade threw up his arms but kept walking.

"Comes with the territory? It might come with *your* territory, but there's nothing about being an NSA analyst that includes being overwhelmed with the smell of formaldehyde."

Kyle pulled him through the door. "Don't worry big guy. I'll catch you in case you faint. And as a special treat, we'll go out for fried-oyster po-boy sandwiches later. I get so hungry after these things."

"Hungry? I doubt I'll want to eat for a week," Cade said.

Upon entering the lab, the smell hit them head on. The odor was a mixture of formaldehyde, rotted chicken, and a stale McDonald's Quarter Pounder with fries. Cade stopped cold.

"Come on, buddy," Kyle said.

The doctor's back was to them and her hands were wrist-deep in the chest cavity of a deceased male whose pasty-white skin was offset against the ebony of hers.

"Dr. Canray, we are with the—" Jana started.

"FBI, I know," the doctor said without looking up. "What can I help you with?"

Cade's eyes fixated on the ghostly white corpse.

"We really do hate to disturb you," Jana said. "We're here investigating the murder of Sheriff Chalmette."

"Murder? Since when does the FBI get involved in murder? Are you with behavioral sciences?"

"No, ma'am. Ma'am? Can we speak confidentially?"

For the first time the doctor looked up.

"What do you think I am a . . . of course we can talk confidentially." The doctor continued her work then said, "You're that FBI agent, aren't you? The one that stopped the bomber in Kentucky."

Jana did not answer.

The doctor continued. "Your mother raised you to be very direct, didn't she? My mother was tough as nails, she was. And what other way to be is there?"

"Yes, ma'am. I was raised to be direct. My grandfather saw to that."

"And this one standing behind me," she said, referring to Kyle. "A real lady killer I bet. But that one over there, he doesn't look so good."

Jana looked at Cade. "Well you're right about Cade. He's turning a lovely shade of green. Not exactly accustomed to this type of thing. But Kyle here? No, ma'am. He's not a lady killer. Instead, he reminds me of an old hand that worked on my grandpa's farm."

"How so?"

"He'd been kicked in the head by a mule, twice," Jana said.

Kyle shook his head. "I'll not grace that with a response."

"What we're interested in is any ballistic evidence that was recovered. We understand the shell casing was found at the scene, but was there a bullet as well?"

"Will Chalmette and I had worked together for years." She stopped a moment. "I hated doing that autopsy. In my job, I enjoy the luxury of almost never knowing the people I work on. No, no bullet was recovered. Will was shot in the head. The shell casing found at the scene indicated a caliber of 7.62 mm. But we were unable to make a match against any known crimes. A bullet like that travels so fast, it just passed right through."

The color retreated from Cade's face and he put his hand over his mouth.

"Believe me," the doctor said, "they searched high and low for the bullet that struck him, or any fragments. But found nothing."

"Don't you find that strange?" Kyle said. "It would seem unusual that they couldn't locate any part of the bullet."

The doctor did not look up from her work. "Yes, I would've expected those baby-blue eyes of yours to ask that question."

Jana shook her head. "But you barely glanced at him. How did you know Kyle had blue eyes?"

"Don't know. I've always known things about people. I guess he just sounds like he has dreamy blue eyes. Like this guy on the table here, Calvin Johnston, age seventy-eight. Found him in his house. No one really knew how he died. That's where I come in. But I could've told you he had brown eyes before I checked. Anyway, getting back to the bullet, the forensic investigators will tell you that sometimes a bullet changes direction after it strikes its target. The bullet could have angled off its initial trajectory. It likely angled up and flew past the sheriff's department, off into the woods. It could be a quarter mile from the scene. No, I'm sorry. We'll never find that bullet. I might have something that can help you though. But now that we're on the subject, tell me why you're so interested in the bullet in particular. After all, finding the shell casing was a lucky break. Lucky in that the killer left it behind, that is. That shell casing amounts to a fingerprint of the firearm. I'm assuming you had hoped that if we recovered the bullet, we could match it against another murder?"

Jana said. "Yes, ma'am. In fact, we have some other questions about the bullet, but if there is no way to locate it, I don't think we'll ever get an answer to those."

For once, the doctor turned and looked at her. "What other questions?"

"As I said, ma'am, this information needs to stay between us. This conversation can't leave this room. Ma'am, it appears that there is a direct relationship between this murder and the murder of FBI Director Stephen Latent. I'm sorry I can't be more specific, but certain evidence recovered at both scenes ties the two together, without a doubt. One thing I can share with you is that, in the case of Director Latent, the arrow that was used to kill him was fired from a crossbow. The broadhead of the arrow was removed and examined. It had been hollowed out and some evidence purposely stuffed inside. What we're wondering is if evidence would have been embedded inside the bullet in this case as well."

"I've covered a lot of murders. I've never heard of anything like that. But like I said a moment ago, I might be able to help you. We may not have the bullet that killed Will Chalmette, but we do have the one that killed the truck driver."

"The truck driver?" Kyle whispered to himself. "There was a bullet recovered from his body? Why didn't you tell us?"

She looked at him. "You didn't ask. But not from his body, from the driver's side door of the truck. The bullet passed through the passenger door and entered the lateral thoracic wall at number eight, his rib cage. Anyway, then it angled down and stopped in the driver's side door. Forensic analysis didn't yield a match to any known or unsolved murders on record."

Cade averted his gaze, but said, "When were you going to tell us about this? We just got finished talking about the sheriff's murder. Why didn't you mention it then?"

The doctor smirked. "Oh, don't worry. I was just waiting to see if blue eyes over here was going to get around to asking about it. I like the way he talks. He's got that kind of south Georgia accent going on, you know?"

"You really are one of a kind, aren't you?" Jana said. "So where is the bullet now?"

"Oh it's back here somewhere. Came back this morning from the forensic lab in New Orleans. They didn't find anything unusual. Want to take a look?"

"Yes, please," Jana said.

The doctor removed her rubber gloves and draped them across the body, then walked to a storage area. When she reemerged, she held a small paper bag with an evidence label on the side. She walked to a lab table, opened the bag, and poured the contents out. A single bullet spilled into a sterile dish.

The bullet was characteristic of one having been fired from a high-powered rifle. Groove marks were etched into its side from where it traveled down the barrel. The front half of the bullet formed into a mushroom shape after having expanded upon impact with the truck and its driver. The bottom half of the lead bullet was encased in heavy brass.

Jana said, "Do you have a dissecting microscope we could look closer with?"

"Sure, honey. Now you're talking my language."

Jana examined the bullet under the high-powered magnification, followed by Kyle.

"See," the doctor said, "there's nothing unusual."

Kyle said to Jana, "Sometimes the brass casing around the base of a bullet gets separated. But not in this case."

The doctor said, "Yes, sometimes. It typically happens in less expensive ammunition. High-grade stuff like this though, you never see separation."

Jana said, "The casing sometimes gets separated? Wait a minute. Looking at the base of the bullet, there is obviously no hole drilled into it, but what if the killer first separated the brass from the lead, and drilled into just the lead portion of the bullet, then put the two pieces back together before firing?"

Kyle nodded. "That's a great question."

"Doctor, can we separate the brass base from the lead body of the bullet?" Jana knew that if the answer was no, she would simply commandeer the evidence and take it to the FBI crime lab for immediate analysis. But getting to the answer quickly was more important than bulling her way past a local official.

"It's a highly unusual request," the doctor said. "But, this bullet has already gone through forensic analysis. They always record digital images of all evidence, so I suppose it couldn't hurt. In doing this, we are definitely going to damage the evidence, but I think, with the photographic documentation already in place, we should be fine." From a drawer she withdrew two pairs of stainless-steel, surgical-grade pliers. "We normally use tools like these to remove a bullet from a body, not separate one in half."

They watched as the doctor applied both sets of pliers to the bullet and began to twist. Within a moment, the lead portion of the bullet separated from the brass base and a few items spilled into the petri dish.

"Look at that!" Cade said.

28

A SHOT IN THE DARK

Office of the Coroner, Saint Tammany Parish

"What the hell *is* that?" Jana said.

The doctor studied the items.

"Well that sure wasn't put there by the factory. Someone planted this. It looks like a grain of wheat, if I'm not mistaken. I'm not sure what this other grain is, but it looks like a seed of grass or barley or something. And this mixture of liquids, maybe it's just me but it almost looks oily."

Kyle squinted at the items. "Kind of congealed together. And what's that? That looks like a flea. Am I right? Doctor, can we get this analyzed immediately?"

"And we don't have time to send it to the FBI crime lab," Jana said.

"Well," Dr. Canray replied, "I'll have to call technicians over at our crime lab. Then we'll have to get this to them."

"How long will it take us to get there?" Cade said.

"Oh, about thirty seconds. The crime lab is right next door."

Jana said, "And you said this wasn't a small town."

"Well, I lied, sort of. We're so close to the hustle and bustle of New Orleans, but we pretend to be a small community. It just doesn't seem to work out that way."

Kyle interrupted. "Does the lab have the capability to analyze this material?"

The doctor looked at him. "Yes. What do you think we are? A bunch of hicks?"

"You'll have to excuse Kyle," Jana said. "He tends to get a little excited about things."

"Do not."

Cade smirked at him.

Thirty minutes later as the analysis commenced, they stood at a long glass window and looked into the sterile laboratory facility. The technician was covered from head to toe with a white jumpsuit and face mask. He separated the items into different petri dishes and ran each into a TRACE 1310 Gas Chromatograph machine. It didn't take long before the technician flashed them a thumbs-up as the last sample passed through. He pointed over their shoulders to a computer screen mounted on the cinder-block wall behind them.

The screen displayed the results of the lab tests. As they studied the output, it was apparent there were four items detected.

"She was right," Kyle said as he read from the monitor.

Wheat (*Triticum monococcum*)

Barley (*Hordeum vulgare*)

Red Wine (*Vitis vinifera*)

Olive Oil (*Olea europaea*)

Flea (*Xenopsylla cheopis*)

Jana shook her head. "This isn't getting easier, it's getting harder. What are we supposed to do with this? I can't get the thought out of my head that Jarrah is laughing at us."

"We are off the mark on this one." Cade said. "And we're not just missing something, we don't even know where to begin.

We've got to figure this out and fast. We all know Jarrah is planning something big. He's leading up to it, he always does."

"Wheat, barley, wine, and oil?" Jana said. "A flea? What the hell does that mean?" She turned and paced the hallway. "Other than the flea, it sounds like something out of the Catholic sacraments."

"Hey," Kyle said, "that's right. Remember when Jarrah questioned if you'd ever gone to church?"

"Yeah. He said, didn't you go to church as a little girl."

"There must be something there," Kyle said. "Let's get this evidence over to the FBI crime lab. They may be able to analyze it further and come up with other clues. In the meantime, does anybody have any ideas? These things we keep finding aren't ringing any bells."

"I agree," Cade said. "They're not ringing any bells with me either. Let's get on a call with Uncle Bill and tell him what we found. Maybe he and Knuckles have something. At this point, I don't think we can take this investigation any further. Let's head back to NSA headquarters."

Jana placed a call and explained the new evidence.

Bill replied, "We couldn't be sure you'd find anything, but you made it pay off. Good work."

"Bill, we're heading to the airport. Have the pilot getting ready to go wings up. We will see you in about two hours," Jana said.

"Not so fast. You're getting on that jet all right, but you're not heading back here. You're going to California. You're not going to believe what we found."

29

NARROWING DOWN A KILLER

En route to the Greater Saint Tammany Regional Airport

Jana's phone vibrated in her pocket, but when Cade saw the look on her face he said, "Jana, what is it?"

In a frantic set of hand motions, she waved Cade and Kyle closer and tilted the phone so they could hear.

"A blocked phone number. It's him," she whispered.

"Jana Baker?" she said

"But, Miss Baker. You knew it was me calling, didn't you?" Jarrah said.

"As a matter of fact, just as the phone rang, a certain stench wafted through the air. So yes, I knew it was you."

"Did your mother not teach you any manners before she was gone? Oh, that's right, you were young. She was never there for you."

"Jarrah, why is it you get so much pleasure in other people's pain? Did mommy not love *you* enough when you were growing up in Syria?"

"It was my father who taught me manners. Yours should have done the same, but he wasn't around either, was he? And to answer your question about pain, it's not that I enjoy inflicting pain on others, it's that I enjoy inflicting pain on you. Your FBI director, your hiking friend, and now I see you've found the untimely demise of a certain old family friend."

"Fuck you, Jarrah!" Jana said.

"Do you realize how easy it would be for me to kill you?"

"If you wanted to kill me, you would have done it in Spain when you murdered my friend Gilda. No," Jana continued, "I think you are enjoying this all too much. I think killing me would make you yawn. What fun would it be without an adversary?"

"An adversary is a person to admire. You, however, have not proven yourself worthy of my admiration."

Jana's hand began to shake. "That's not how I see it. When I hunted down, then shot, your first disciple, Shakey Kunde, he squealed like a little girl."

"Do not test my patience, Miss Baker. I might change my mind about killing you. But we both know Shakey did no such thing. You are correct that you stopped me on my first attempt, but perhaps you are forgetting my second, the scorched earth and molten metal that used to be the headquarters of the CIA, the beast itself. It has been fun watching the news coverage over the last year since I detonated a nuclear device there. Such a large swath of the landscape now turned into gray ash."

"Is this why you called me? To taunt and boast about your pathetic accomplishments?"

"Oh you know far better than that, Miss Baker. You know my calls have a purpose, and torturing you with them is simply a side benefit, a perk, you might say."

"More riddles for us, Jarrah? More lies, misdirection? Which one is it this time?"

"You think everything I tell you is a distraction meant to send you the wrong way? Is that what you think?"

"You went to a lot of trouble to misdirect us with the nuclear weapon you detonated. Which reminds me, Shakey Kunde's little brother squealed like a little girl when he died too."

"The younger brother proved most useful in diverting you from the true location of the nuclear device. He was a martyr, a hero of Allah. And he sits with him now. Think of the glory, Miss Baker. To have pleased your God with such magnificence."

Kyle looked at Jana's trembling hand and nodded to Cade.

Jana's volume erupted and her breathing became erratic. "Magnificence? You had a suicide bomber murder hundreds of thousands of innocent people. He isn't sitting on the right hand of God, he's burning in hell!"

The sound of Jarrah's voice became distant, as if he had pulled the phone away from his mouth. "I am become death, a destroyer of worlds." His voice emboldened now. "Your inventor of the nuclear weapon, Robert Oppenheimer, had such brilliant words." His tone deepened and reminded Jana of the sound of grinding metal. "It is near, Miss Baker. The time is near. I am close to completing my final objective and you are far behind."

Jana's breathing shallowed and Kyle moved behind to catch her if she blacked out.

"What do you mean you are near?" she said. "Near to what? If I am so far behind in the game, it can't hurt to tell me now."

"The sun has been strong on my face in this part of your country. I've been here for many days, readying my next glorious success."

"Spit it out, Waseem. Are you planning to detonate another device on American soil?"

"Of course I am, and you know I can do it. You know much of this story. There were ten original warheads. Two I used last year, two were recaptured by the Australians, two more were reported destroyed when Russians bombed my old stomping grounds, the Hindu Kush mountains, and the other four? Well, one never knows where they might be. But I tell you this. You will see the results of one shortly."

Jana's heart rate increased. "You sold at least three more."

"Surely it must be frustrating. You have not been able to track the location of the other warheads, nor any source of funding I received when I sold them. I have all the funds I will ever need. Funds that my followers will use to carry on attacks long after I am gone."

"Long after you are gone?" Jana said. "You said the sun was strong on your face. Where are you? Florida, Texas, California?"

"Oh, California. Such a beautiful place. It will be such a shame, so much beautiful country. And to think Allah lets you live on this land. The thought disgusts me. In fact, I believe Allah will be overjoyed when I vaporize the land, liberating it from such filthy pigs."

Jana's grip on Kyle's shoulder tightened. "California? Where in California?"

"I'm not going to give it away so easily, Miss Baker. You have to figure the rest out for yourself based on the clues I have left. My only hope is that you will be on-site when the device detonates. The last thing I will say is this. *Where this device is set will cause more destruction than any other spot in the land.*" The line went dead.

"Jarrah? Shit! He hung up. California, oh my God. We can't evacuate the entire state. Where is he going to hit? We've got to get on the phone with Uncle Bill."

Cade leaned forward. "He said we could figure it out based on the clues he's already given us. Dammit, we need the lab results from all of the evidence, and we need to see it in total."

"Come on," Kyle said. "We've got to get on that plane and head to California. Uncle Bill must've found something important. He already knew where Jarrah's next target would be. Let's go!"

Moments after the plane went wheels up, they were on a secure conference with Uncle Bill and Knuckles at NSA headquarters.

"Bill," Kyle said, "what have you got? How did you know we were supposed to go to California? We just talked to Waseem Jarrah. He called Jana again. He specifically told us California was the target."

"I'll tell you how I know in just a second. But what kind of target? What did he say?"

Jana leaned in. "It's *nuclear*, Bill. He's threatening to detonate another device. He said last year when he stole the nuclear missile, they divided the warhead into its ten separate parts. He sold seven of them which is why he has so much cash on hand. One he used to detonate in North Korea, the other at CIA headquarters. It's the last one, Bill. He's got one more. We never knew if he sold it or was saving it for himself. California is the target, but he wouldn't say where. He did say, though, that the device would detonate in the place that would cause more destruction than any place in the land."

Cade said, "That can help us narrow it down a little further as to the location, but not by much. It's the evidence, I'm telling you. He's leaving us clues at all the murder scenes to communicate something. What have you found?"

"The strongest clues from the evidence collected at Stephen Latent's assassination relate to the figs and the wasp. But first the stone. It's a piece of rose quartz. Probably from Spain, a mountain called El Yelmo."

"Wait," Cade said, "isn't rose quartz common? How do you know it's from Spain?"

"Soil and pollen contaminants were on it. In fact, the stone itself probably originated at El Yelmo, but it's where the stone likely journeyed next that's interesting."

"And where is that?" Jana said.

Bill continued. "You were hiking the Camino trial, Jana. The large stone pile at Cruz de Ferro, it's from there. Soil contaminants are a spot-on match, and pollen grains."

Jana nodded in recognition.

"Knuckles, you have the lab report on the pollen grains?" Bill said.

"Yes, sir," he said. "*Elaeagnus angustifolia, Fraxinus ornus,* and *Platanus hispanica*, all native trees and plants that surround the area."

"Cruz de what? What's that?" Cade asked.

"Cruz de Ferro," Jana said. "Look, all along the Camino trail, people leave stones. They're everywhere. Along trails, on headstones, they're laid down in the shape of arrows to point the way, and especially at Cruz de Ferro. It's like a shrine. There's a tall pole there with a cross at the top. Everyone that hikes the trail brings a stone from home to leave there, at the base of the cross. The pile is huge, probably thirty feet high."

"Why do people leave stones?" Cade said.

"I don't know, Cade," Jana said with a hint of frustration in her voice. "We all did it. Stones are kind of permanent, like you're leaving something lasting behind. People have done it for so long, it makes you feel a part of it all." A distant gaze painted her face. "For a lot of us it's different. We carry a stone from our homes that represents something we've been carrying around inside us. Something we want to let go of. Part of hiking that trail is coming to grips with something you need to let go of. And we leave it at the base of the cross."

"Okay, I'm sorry," Cade said, "I didn't know."

Jana said, "Gilda and Latent. Jarrah left evidence at both murder scenes to point toward his next victim. God I miss her."

Cade said, "Bill, what about the fig and wasp?"

"I can't wait to hear this one," Jana said.

"We did genetic testing on both the fig pulp and the wasp to identify them down to the species. They are interrelated. These type of fig trees live in two distinct regions in the world. They originate in the Middle East and did not exist anywhere else until the mid-1800s when they were imported to California. And they're only grown in a very limited region there. The wasp is a species known as *Blastophaga psenes*."

"So what's the relationship between the two?" Kyle said.

It was Knuckles who answered. "It's got to do with the history of the fig trees when they were first brought to California. The Californian farmers couldn't figure out why the trees weren't germinating. It took them a long time, but they finally figured out that they needed a particular wasp to pollinate the trees. Without the wasp, the fig fruit grows but is inedible. So, they started importing those wasps and releasing them around their fig orchards. After that, they had successful crops."

"Okay," Jana said, "so what are you saying? Jarrah is telegraphing the location of his major attack by indicating the region of California where these fig trees grow?"

"That's exactly what I'm saying," Knuckles said, still proud of his earlier commentary on the nuances of fig fertilization.

Cade shook his head. "But wait a minute. How big of a region in California are these trees grown? Does it narrow it down any?"

Silence and the shuffling of feet were all that could be heard across the phone line.

"Bill?" Jana said.

"Well, that's the problem."

"How big of a problem?"

"About half a million acres running for miles up and down California."

30

AN IMPROBABLE THEORY

On board a Gulfstream Six. Altitude 7,300 feet. Airspeed 376 knots. Seventy-three nautical miles west-north-west of New Orleans, Louisiana

Jana put her fingers into her hair. "So how are we supposed to narrow it down?"

Bill said, "I'm getting too old for this shit."

"Where?" Jana screamed. "Where is he going to hit?"

"That's anyone's guess," Knuckles said. "Looking at it on the map, the fig orchards run for miles. He could hit anywhere along there."

"We've got to find out, and right now. We can't guess! We have to stop him."

Cade unbuckled his seatbelt and placed his hands in hers.

"Jana, calm down. We're all under a lot of stress here."

Jana's chest heaved in an effort to vacuum in enough oxygen, and her face began to pale. "And that's not all," she said. "It's *misdirection*. I'm telling you, he's purposely misleading us. He's going to get us off chasing the wind while he detonates a nuclear device somewhere else."

Her head began to shake, the effect similar to a person with

Parkinson's Disease. "I can't take this not knowing. I can't take it!"

Cade grabbed her shoulders. "You need to look me in the eye. Don't slip away now." But it was too late, her PTSD went into hyperdrive. Jana's eyes rolled into the back of her head and her body began convulsing.

"Kyle! Grab her legs! Don't let her thrash around."

"What's going on?" Uncle Bill yelled into the phone. "Is she okay? What's happening?"

"Jana, stay with us," Kyle said. "Jana!"

"Dammit, Bill," Kyle said as he held Jana's legs, "I told you something like this would happen."

Cade glared up at him. "What do you mean you told Bill something like this would happen?"

"Look at her, Cade!" Kyle belted. "She's a danger to herself and a danger to us. She's going to get someone killed."

"Screw you, Kyle!"

"Hey!" Uncle Bill yelled across the phone. "You two get ahold of yourselves. We've got a man down. Now what's happening?"

The rigidity began to abate from Jana's muscles and light started returning to her eyes.

"She's coming around," Kyle said. "Listen, let's take a break. It will be two hours before we touch down. We'll call you back in a little while, once we get settled. And, Bill?"

"Yes, Kyle."

"We can talk about this offline."

"I know what you're going to say, Kyle," Bill replied.

"And let's have a rundown of all the evidence. I mean everything. The evidence hidden inside the bullet and broadhead, the glass beads, everything we've got. There's a pattern here and we're missing it."

"Agreed. Talk to you in a bit." The phone line went dead.

Jana's color returned to her face and she sat upright.

"You okay?" Cade said. "You scared us there."

"I'm fine. Dammit, I thought I was past this."

"It's the job, Jana. This job is killing you."

"It's not the job, Cade. It's the asshole."

Kyle scowled. "So you think getting rid of Waseem Jarrah will make your PTSD episodes go away?"

"Bet my life on it." Jana stared out a port-side window onto a mountain range below, then said, "He's misleading us."

"I hear what you're saying, but we have to go with what we have," Kyle said.

"I'm with Kyle on this one," Cade said. "And, Jana, think about it. Let's say you're right and we're being misled. My question would be, what else would we do right now? I mean, if we have absolutely no idea what other direction to take, we have to pursue the leads we currently have. You never know, but I think he's leading us in the correct direction."

"Why?" came her whispered reply.

Cade studied her face, then said, "Like you said earlier, he'd want to keep the game close."

"Maybe you're right," Jana said. "But he's never wanted to keep us close in the past. He's wanted to send us in the wrong direction. This is the last of his nuclear warheads. He's already detonated one in the United States, which means he's accomplished his lifelong goal. If this one doesn't go off, he'll be pissed, but he's always got the first one to look back on."

But Jana's thoughts trailed back to her suspicion that Waseem Jarrah was misleading them. In the previous attack, he used a second jihadist as a decoy to carry a backpack containing radioactive material. The material was meant to leave a trail that would be detected by Geiger counters. The entire investigative team, including FBI and NSA, had taken the bait.

The real bomb had been parked half a mile from CIA headquarters. And since the blast radius of the device was one mile in diameter, the entire facility was destroyed. It was a failure of epic proportions and hundreds of thousands of Americans had lost their lives in the process.

"And it's not just misdirection I'm worried about. Remember what he said? He said he would detonate in the place that would cause the most destruction."

"Right," Cade said, "in California. The most destruction in California."

Jana looked at him but her eyes wandered, as if she was entranced in a thought that would not abate.

Half an hour later they accessed a secure satellite uplink to NSA headquarters and initiated a video conference from the plane with Uncle Bill, Knuckles, and a dozen other analysts.

"All right, Bill," Jana said, "let's have a rundown of all known evidence. There's so many details, and new information you've apparently just discovered from the crime lab. We've got to piece it together." Jana cocked her head at Bill. "Bill, what are you smiling at?"

"Oh, nothing. Just thinking about the first time I met you."

"And?"

"That was a green FBI agent, full of fire and vinegar, eager to prove herself."

"I'm not sure I want to hear the rest of that thought. And now?"

"Now, a leader. Still full of fire and vinegar, of course."

"Thanks, Bill, I think," Jana said as she laughed. "Knuckles, are you doing the briefing?"

"Yes, ma'am. I mean, yes Jana. Okay, on the monitor I've

listed the evidence we've collected so far. Number one. Director Latent was killed with a crossbow. The broadhead on the arrow that killed him had been hollowed out and filled with the pulp of a fig." He repeated what Uncle Bill had already told them about the figs. "We did further analysis and determined that this particular fig came from the California orchards, not from the Middle East."

"Thanks for the recap, professor," Cade said.

"Wait," Jana said, "how do you know? How do you know the fig in question came from California?"

"The lab doesn't lie. Pesticide residue, pH of the soil, salinity, pollen grains, and pollutants. They all are a spot-on match to this region right here," Knuckles said as he pointed at a spot on the map of California. "Although this species of fig can be grown in most of the state, these soil properties are a match for this region, just outside of San Francisco and San Jose."

"Wait," Kyle said, "are you thinking he's going to target San Francisco?"

Uncle Bill said, "People, let's stay on point. We need to see all the evidence in total before we rush to judgment on where the next target might be."

"As I was saying," Knuckles said, "the lab has pinpointed the region where that fig was grown. It might be significant, it might not. But let's not forget, we also recovered a glass bead at the scene. This one contained a tiny figurine of a man riding a horse and carrying a bow. Now the bow might signify something, or it might just be that Director Latent was assassinated with a bow—we don't know."

Jana rubbed the uppermost bullet scar on her torso and her eyes took on a distant gaze. She was entranced in a memory. "Oh, it means something."

"Number two. Jana's friend Gilda. Gilda von Horscht. Ms. von Horscht was killed in Spain, stabbed through the heart with a sword. We believe the killer was Waseem Jarrah himself. A glass bead was found embedded in the chest cavity. The bead also contained a tiny figurine of a man riding a horse. This horseman was carrying a sword. Again, the sword could be significant in that Miss von Horscht was murdered with a sword, or maybe not."

Bill glanced at Jana then cleared his throat. "No need to be so graphic, son."

"Sorry," Knuckles muttered.

"And what else have you found about this one?" Kyle said.

"There was something else found inside the body cavity of Miss von Horscht."

Jana crossed her arms and sat down.

"It was a leaf, a fig leaf. Soil toxins, pesticides, pH level, everything is a match to the exact fig found inside the broadhead at Director Latent's assassination." He continued. "The leaf was also covered in a powder. The lab says it's *Chicorium intybus*, roasted chicory root."

Jana's hand moved to her forehead. "Chicory. New Orleans. Shit, he telegraphed he was going to that area for his next murder by leaving us evidence that pointed in that direction."

"I don't get that one," Cade said. "What's roasted chicory root used for? And what's that got to do with New Orleans?"

It was Jana who answered. "When I was a kid at Christmas, Willy Chalmette would bring my mom a can of chicory coffee from New Orleans. In fact, when I was little, Mom took me there one time, to the French Quarter. There's a place called Café du Monde. It's old and really famous for chicory coffee and beignets. And before you ask me what those are, they're like a fried pastry covered in powdered sugar. They're heaven in your mouth is what they are. Anyway, I always remembered the cafe because Willy pointed out this busboy to us. He was this little old man cleaning tables. Willy said he could remember the same guy having worked there from thirty years ago."

Knuckles shifted in his seat. He had found more information about chicory and looked as though it would erupt from him if he did not start speaking soon. "Chicory was grown in France. In the early 1800s, when Napolean initiated a blockade, the French were deprived of their coffee imports, and turned to roasted chicory as a substitute. When the blockade finally ended, people has become accustomed to the taste and continued using it. Other areas of French influence, like New Orleans, continued as well."

"Again," Cade said, "thanks, professor. Is there anything else, not related to chicory, that might help us?"

"The sword used to kill Miss von Horscht may be significant. The Spanish secret service says the wounds inflicted on Miss Gilda are a direct match to a sword recently stolen from the Museo Nacional del Prado, the largest museum in Spain. The sword, and a knife that was also stolen, were believed to date back to the time of Mohammad and the prophets. In fact, both objects are believed to have been owned *by the Prophet Mohammad himself.*"

"Hold on a minute, professor," Cade said. "You're telling me the sword that was used to kill Gilda was actually owned by Mohammad? As in the Koran's Prophet Mohammad?"

"That's exactly what I'm telling you. Here's what we know about it. It, in particular, is said to be one of the original nine swords that Mohammad owned. The other eight are in museums as well. This one is known as *Al-Battar*, apparently taken by

Muhammad as booty from the Banu Qaynaqa, one of the three main Jewish tribes living in seventh-century Medina, modern-day Saudi Arabia. This one is called the 'sword of the prophets' and is inscribed in Arabic with the names of several key players in the Bible. David, Solomon, Moses, Aaron, Joshua, Zechariah, John, Muhammad himself, and," Knuckles paused a moment, "Jesus."

Jana turned her head toward the monitor. "Jarrah killed Gilda with a sword that has the name of Jesus on it?"

"There's more."

"Go on," Jana said.

"It's the only one of the original nine swords that wasn't housed in a museum that sits in an Islamic country."

Uncle Bill nodded. "Perhaps Jarrah was pissed off that the historic sword belonged in his homeland in the first place. And perhaps the origin or timeframe of the sword has significance as well."

"Why does Knuckles look like he's not done talking about the sword?" Jana said.

Knuckles exhaled. "This particular sword is claimed by some to be the actual sword that Jesus will use when he returns to earth to defeat the Antichrist."

"The sword Jesus will use?" Jana let the thought play forward in her mind. "Jarrah murdered Gilda with a sword Mohammad stole from the Jews, that will one day be used by Jesus when he returns? He's laughing at us."

Cade said, "He knows we'll find these details. Jarrah went to an enormous amount of trouble to set this up."

Jana said, "I'm telling you. He's laughing at us, and he's spitting on Christianity. *Now* tell me that the figurines of horsemen don't have significance."

"No argument here," Uncle Bill said. "Let's get to the other evidence."

"Third. Sheriff Will Chalmette, assassinated in Louisiana, in Saint Tammany Parish, just north of New Orleans. The sheriff was killed with a sniper rifle. The bullet that killed him was never recovered, but the first round fired struck a semi-trailer and killed the driver. It was recovered. The base of the bullet was found to be hollowed out, similarly to the broadhead. Inside was a strange concoction of items: wheat, barley, oil, wine, and a single flea. Chemical residue from each of these are all traceable back to exactly where they were grown and produced. Except the flea, of course."

Jana wrapped her arms around her torso and she rocked back and forth.

Cade watched, fearing another post-traumatic stress episode might ensue at any moment.

"What's the flea supposed to mean?" Jana said.

"Wait," Kyle said, "all four of the items were grown in the same place?"

Knuckles pointed back to the map of California. "Same region as the fig orchards. Same soil contaminants, pollutants, everything."

"He's got to be telegraphing his intent," Uncle Bill said. "He's going to target this area."

Jana again repeated, this time in a whisper, "He's misleading us."

"Well, he's going to an awful lot of trouble to point us here. The soil-toxin profile on all four items points to crops grown right here, not far from San Francisco. The figs, wheat, and barley, the olives, and even the grapes used to produce the wine were all grown right here."

"You could be right," Kyle said, "and I hear what you're saying about trace elements found in the soil, but all this stuff points back to the Middle East as well. Think about it. Everything so far could symbolize that region."

"But there's one more thing that points Sheriff Chalmette's murder to San Francisco," Knuckles said. "The bullet itself had traces of something else on it. Chlorophyll, chlorophyll from the leaf of a plant, a fig plant. The same fig plant."

"Drawing us away," Jana whispered.

"What did you say?" Cade said as he put his hand on her shoulder. There was no reply. "Jana, you're shaking like a leaf. Stand up, maybe it will help if you move around a little bit."

Knuckles continued. "And the glass bead found at the scene was a little different as well. The bead was coated in sulfuric acid, apparently used to cover any trace evidence on its surface. This one contained a figurine of a man riding a horse, but this time, the horseman wasn't carrying any weapon. He was carrying a set of what appear to be scales. We're assuming at this point they represent the scales of justice."

Jana stood but her shoulders rounded over. "Why would he bother with the sulfuric acid?"

"What do you mean, Jana?" Kyle said. "He's covering any trace evidence that we might have found on the exterior of the glass beads."

"That's my point. Why bother with that when you're telegraphing exactly where you want us to go? He's placing figs and wasps and olive oil and all kinds of shit right in our hands for us to analyze. Those things are pointing us to California. And then there's the other things, the stone from the Camino trail, the chicory coating everything found in Gilda, and now this flea. One set of evidence is pointing us to California, the other set points from one murder victim to the next. Then there's the glass beads. I still don't know what they point to. So why bother covering up trace evidence?"

"I hadn't considered that," Bill said as his fingers found their way into the depths of his beard. "Anyone care to advance a theory?"

Even Knuckles looked like a lost puppy. At last, Jana looked directly into the monitor. "We're forgetting about the other assassin. We knew Jarrah must have had help. After all, Stephen Latent was assassinated at the same time Jarrah was with me in Spain." Her eyes trailed off, out one of the airplane windows. "When he murdered Gilda and stuffed a glass bead and a fig leaf into her chest." She knelt to the floor and continued squeezing her arms around herself as she rocked back and forth.

Cade knelt with her.

"The assassin," Bill said. "The assassin was covering *his* tracks, not Jarrah's. The assassin wouldn't want anything to trace back to him. That's why he used the sulfuric acid."

"Well," Knuckles said, "we know nothing of him. Nothing. And even that is an assumption. Calling him a *him*, I mean."

"He'd be a contractor," Kyle said. "A hired gun with the kind of connections to be in association with Waseem Jarrah."

"There was that one guy from the last time," Cade said. "Remember? When the investigation trailed the source of the nuclear weapon that detonated at CIA. There was mention of a contractor Jarrah had likely used. His name was Rafael."

"Right," Knuckles said. "Rafael. More of a ghost than anything else. There's not even a photo of him. We don't even know if he's real."

"He's got to be real," Uncle Bill said. "Even if our intel is wrong on his name, there was definitely a contractor involved last year in transporting the suicide bomber and two nuclear warheads. One of the bombs was shipped to North Korea, and the most likely originator of that shipment was a contractor known only as Rafael."

Jana said, "So that's it, three dead people, three separate sets of clues. Bill, how are we going to know when he's finished?"

Bill looked over his glasses. "Finished? You mean finished giving us evidence?"

Jana nodded her head. "There would have to be a start and a finish. It would lead us right up to his main event, whatever Jarrah has planned. How are we supposed to know if he has finished delivering evidence to us?"

Kyle added, "Evidence in the form of fresh bodies."

"Well," Knuckles said, "we've got a lot to work with here. Three assassinations, three glass beads, all with a figurine of a horse with a rider, carrying something. I guess I'm saying I don't know when we will know if he's finished."

Through the video monitor, the trio watched as a woman in the NSA command center with soft brunette hair walked toward Uncle Bill. "Sir, I think you should look at this," she said.

Bill studied the paper, then rubbed his eyes. "Not three assassinations, four. This one out of Atlanta. It looks like he's taken out the director of the Center for Disease Control."

"What?" Jana yelled.

Bill flustered. "The director of the CDC was apparently murdered. Don't shoot the messenger."

A flood of emotions overwhelmed Jana and she began to sob. "I can't take it anymore. I can't take it."

Cade held onto her. "Jana, what's wrong? Do you know the director of the CDC?"

"Kathy. Her name is Kathy Whelan." She shook her head then

choked out, "She was my mom's college roommate. I remember her coming to the house a lot when I was a kid. But it was later, after mom died, that I remember her most. She and mom were really close. My mom's passing devastated her. After that, Aunt Kathy, as I used to call her, kind of looked after me. My grandmother had passed away and I had no women in my life. She did her best to fill that gap. She even loaned me the money to go to college. I didn't finish paying her back until about the time I went to training at Quantico."

No one spoke as they all tried to comprehend the enormity of Jana's losses.

"I am going to kill him," Jana whispered.

Bill looked back at the paper. "No gunshot wounds, knife wounds, or anything else that looks like violence. No apparent cause of death."

Knuckles walked to him. "The director of the CDC? I know she's connected to Jana, but how do we know this is related, or even a murder, for that matter?"

"Because of this," Bill said as he turned the paper toward the video monitor. It was a close-up image of a small glass bead. The image was detailed enough to clearly depict the figurine of a man riding a horse. In his hand, the rider carried a sickle. "We may not know how she died just yet, but I'm pretty sure we'll find out soon enough. And to Jana's point, I'm betting it has something to do with the flea found at the sheriff's murder scene. That's the one clue that hasn't fit yet."

"That's four," Knuckles said as he rubbed his neck. "Four people assassinated, four glass beads. All of them with a guy riding a horse. Now what the hell are these damned horsemen supposed to mean?" Knuckles began to pace the floor and speak to himself, entranced in a line of thought. "It's got to have a lot to do with the beads. But not the beads so much, the guys riding horses. So what do we know about that? Four horses, four men riding them. Each carrying something. Four horsemen."

Jana sat upright. "Say that again."

"Say what? Which part?"

"You said horsemen. Four *horsemen*." Jana stood. "Were all the horses different colors?"

Knuckles scowled at the monitor. "Different colors? What does that matter?"

"Were they?" Jana was almost yelling.

"Yes, each horse was a different color, so what?"

"What were the colors of the horses?"

"I don't see what that has to do with—"

"Tell me!" Jana screamed.

"All right, well, yes. Let me look at the evidence sheets again. The first horse at Director Latent's crime scene was white. The second, found inside of Gilda's body, hold on, where is that one? Okay, yes. The second horse was red. The third one, found at the scene with the sheriff in Louisiana, that horse was black. This last one—"

Jana said, "Let me guess. The fourth horse, found at the scene of Kathy's murder, that one was pale white, or possibly pale green, am I right?"

"Pale green." Knuckles stared at her. "How did you know that?"

"And there were dead rats or mice at the murder scene, weren't there? Some kind of rodents?"

"Yes, Miss Baker," Uncle Bill said as he read the evidence report in his hand. "There were several dead rats found at the scene. They don't know what that means. I'd be very interested to know how you knew that."

Jana closed her eyes and her voice became monotone. "The

apocalypse. The Four Horsemen of the Apocalypse. It's from the Bible, the book of Revelations. Pale green was supposed to symbolize the putrid color of death. Each glass bead contains one of the four horseman of the apocalypse. Dammit, why didn't I think of this earlier? And the rodents. Pestilence. I'd bet anything they find some disease or plague to be the cause of death, and it was probably transmitted by fleas. Remember how Jarrah asked me if I went to church as a child? He's taunting us. He's taunting us with our Christian Bible." She looked at the others. "None of you ever studied the Bible? Look, my grandfather taught Sunday school. The book of Revelations is the last chapter in the Bible. It foretells of the end of the world. The Four Horsemen of the Apocalypse are unsealed to more or less announce the coming of the end of the world, each bringing with it a different type of death. Jarrah assassinated these four people in four separate ways, each corresponding to one of the four horsemen of the apocalypse. He's finished. Jarrah is finished giving us evidence. There were only four horsemen in the Bible. We have to piece it all together and figure out what it means, before it's too late. He's ready to start his final act right now."

Kyle slumped into a chair. "You're right. My God, you're right. When I was a kid we learned about it in Sunday school, but you hardly ever hear about the book of Revelations in church anymore."

"Don't look at me," Cade said. "I never went to church as a kid."

"But, Jana," Kyle said. "Even though there were only four horsemen, they all had symbolic meanings. Each of the Four Horsemen was released one at a time, as Jesus opened another seal. The opening of the seals announces the end of the world, but they were foretelling how it would happen. Hold on, let me pull up the Bible passage in the YouVersion app on my phone. Okay, here it is, Revelations 6."

Kyle read from the passage. "'When he opened the fourth seal, I heard the voice of the fourth living creature say, "Come!"' . . . " Kyle looked up. "Jana, Jarrah said that to you on the phone." He continued. "'And I looked, and behold, a pale horse! And its rider's name was *Death*, and Hades followed him. And they were given authority over a fourth of the earth, to kill with sword and with famine and with pestilence and by wild beasts of the earth.'"

Jana said, "Pestilence. The fourth horseman's name was Death. How very appropriate, coming from Jarrah."

"'And hell followed him,'" Kyle added. "Jarrah wants to send us all to hell."

"*To kill with a sword*," Knuckles said. "Jarrah killed Jana's friend with a sword."

Bill scratched his chin through his beard. "To kill with a sword, famine, pestilence, and beasts of the earth. Perhaps we have all that to look forward to."

Kyle read further. "When the fifth seal opens, it mentions an altar, filled with the souls of those who had been slain for the word of God."

"Yeah," Jana said, "these were souls that were martyred for God. They want their revenge but are told to wait because more martyrs will come, and then their numbers will be right."

"Perhaps Jarrah is stacking up the bodies of martyrs," Knuckles said. "In his mind, the numbers will then be right."

"There were four horsemen, but a total of seven seals, right?" Uncle Bill said. "What about the other seals, Kyle?"

Kyle read, "'When he opened the sixth seal, I looked, and behold, there was a great earthquake, and the sun became black as sackcloth, the full moon became like blood, the stars of the sky fell to the earth as the *fig tree* sheds its winter fruit when shaken by a gale.'"

"There's the fig tree," Jana said. "And it specifically says an earthquake."

Kyle continued. "'The sky vanished like a scroll that is being rolled up, and every mountain and island was removed from its place.'" He looked up. "Listen to this part. 'Then the kings of the earth and the great ones and the generals and the rich and the powerful, and everyone, slave and free, hid themselves in the caves and among the rocks of the mountains.'"

"Jarrah would love that," Bill said. "Making us and our leaders hide in fear."

"The seventh seal opens with silence," Kyle said. "Then more destruction. The end of times as we know it."

"The detonation must be what Jarrah would consider the seventh seal," Jana said.

"Uncle Bill?" Knuckles said. "I'm looking at a corresponding passage in the Koran. It says a lot of the same things. It sounds like the Bible and the Koran agree about the end of the world."

"Okay," Uncle Bill said, "let's start working down this path. I want everyone to break out a Bible and go through it. And look up any hidden meanings to anything related to these horsemen. But that's not all, we've still got all these other clues that are pointing us to the San Francisco area. What is he telegraphing? Remember, he's got one nuclear device left. If he detonates inside of San Francisco, and we could've stopped it, I'll never forgive myself. We've got to know where and when he intends to detonate."

Jana looked at Knuckles. "The nuclear device? The ones Jarrah has his hands on. Does it have the same blast radius as the one that took out CIA?"

Knuckles answered, "Yes. All ten original warheads came out of a single Russian ballistic missile. Each has a blast radius of one mile. It would cause utter devastation in downtown San Francisco."

"Okay," Bill said. "You'll be in the air for a while. Let's regroup in an hour. Let me get my people working on it on our end."

"All right, Bill. Talk to you in a bit." Jana disconnected the video call.

"I just . . ." Jana paused as she looked at Cade. "I don't think Jarrah would stop at that. Think about it, this is his last nuclear device. Detonating inside downtown San Francisco wouldn't be enough for him. It's devastation, sure, but it's not enough. How is he going to black out the sky and make the moon look like blood by destroying San Francisco? We not only have to know when he's going to detonate but I still say we've got to determine *where*.We need to think about what would be the best place to detonate. Like he said, the place that would cause the most destruction and death."

"More death than would occur from the blast radius itself?" Kyle said.

"Yes. He'd want to detonate in such a way that the blast would be magnified."

"I'm not sure I follow," Cade said.

"I don't know. I think I've been inside his head for too long. It's starting to get to me. Hey, bring up that map of California that Knuckles was looking at. What else could he hit in that area near San Francisco, where all of those pieces of evidence, the grapes, olive oil, wheat, figs, all that, were grown. Is there anything out there? Any target? I know the entire area is heavily populated, but what are we missing? Where could he detonate and get a magnified effect?"

They all studied the map.

"Well," Cade said, "there are a lot of strips of farmland. These look like grape orchards, and the figs, those are only grown in a tight region. They grow in this area here."

"What's that line running north-south on the map?" Kyle asked. "It borders the whole area we're talking about. Is that a river?"

"Oh my God," Jana said as her eyes widened. "That's no river. That's the San Andreas Fault line."

31

LEADING TO ANYWHERE

Gulfstream Six. Altitude 18,116 feet. Airspeed 796 knots. Twelve nautical miles south-south-west of Las Cruces, New Mexico

"The San Andreas . . ." Jana said. But as the thought played forward in her mind, a cold chill ran up her spine. "What if he detonates somewhere along the fault line? Could he set off an actual earthquake that way? The Bible mentioned an earthquake. That's not possible, right? Sounds like something out of a science fiction novel."

Cade said, "I'm pretty sure that wouldn't work. A nuclear explosion is huge, but the San Andreas Fault runs for something like seven hundred miles. I can't imagine you could set off any type of man-made disruption that could cause the fault line to shift. The thing is enormous. No, I say if he's telegraphing us to San Francisco, we should stay focused on that. Let's not get distracted. We need to look at the city itself and figure out where the most effective place to position the weapon would be."

Kyle said, "We shouldn't leave anything off the table. But you're right about looking for the best location in the city. My biggest concern is that even if we have a good idea of the location to detonate, I'm not sure we could stop him anyway. Remember, these weapons are small enough to fit into a large backpack. They weigh about eighty pounds, plus maybe a few more for a detonator device. A person wearing a backpack could just walk down the street, or get on one of the streetcars that are so common in San Francisco, and detonate. By then it would be too late."

"Pilot?" Kyle yelled. "Take us to SFO."

"Roger that," the pilot replied, then spoke into his radio. The plane began a slow turn to course-correct toward the San Francisco area.

As the minutes ticked by, the group focused on multiple points across the city of San Francisco that would make excellent targets. A nuclear device with enough yield to create a blast radius of one mile in diameter could wreak havoc on anything in its wake. There didn't seem to be a logical place in the city that would be more effective than others.

An hour of flight time later, Jana rubbed her eyes. Everyone on board the Gulfstream jet was head down, studying a map of the city.

When the video monitor blinked to life again, Uncle Bill's voice broke the silence. "Did you find anything?"

Jana didn't look up and instead rubbed her eyes. "Hey, Bill." She pulled the ponytail free of the band holding it in place and her golden hair rolled forward like a silk sheet.

Cade stared at it the way a person stares into a campfire.

"We're touching down at San Francisco International Airport. But, we found more possible targets than I care to admit," she said. "There doesn't seem to be anything in the city itself he would specifically go after, other than mass destruction, that is. Jarrah could put the device anywhere. Downtown would be particularly devastating, but Fisherman's Wharf, Chinatown,

Market Street around the Moscone Center, they're all highly populated, touristy areas. Nothing is jumping out at us."

"Nothing?"

As Jana stood she said, "Well, Bill, we did have this harebrained idea. It provided a bit of amusement in that it was so outlandish."

Bill grinned, although underneath the mass of grizzled facial hair, it was hard to tell. "And what was that? Remember, there are no stupid ideas here."

"It was something about placing the device inside the San Andreas Fault line to cause an earthquake."

When she looked back at Bill, she saw something in his eyes. It was an expression she couldn't quite place. To her, it looked like his brain struggled with two opposing thoughts locked in a battle against one another. The first was fear, but what startled her more was that it was infused with something else: revelation.

"Jana? I think you're at the wrong location."

32

COVERED IN SPADES

715 Gibbons Street in Alexandria, Virginia

The mixed residential, small-business district was reminiscent of so many similar neighborhoods in the Washington, DC, metropolitan area. The residential building was a two-story complex, complete with dormer windows characteristic of the architecture of the neighborhood. The exterior was all brick that alternated in color, the first few condos a natural brick, the next few painted white, then back to brick again.

At 4:58 a.m. the pounding on the front door began. By the time Lyle Branson awakened, it sounded like a stampede of cattle. He looked out his second-floor bedroom window into the strobing of blue lights to see two Ford Crown Victorias, unmarked official vehicles, on the street below.

"What the hell?" Branson said. He stumbled out of bed and down the stairs. "All right, all right," he yelled. "Jesus, I don't even have my pants on." He unbolted and opened the door to find four men in business suits. The first held out a set of FBI credentials.

"This can't be good," Branson said.

"Federal agents. Dr. Lyle Branson?"

"Yes?"

"Dr. Branson, you'll need to get dressed immediately," the agent said. "We're to escort you."

"Escort me? Escort me where? It's not even 5:00 a.m. What is this about?"

"We're not at liberty to say. Please hurry, sir. This is a matter of utmost urgency."

Branson stepped back to let the men in, then closed the door behind them. "You dented my door, you know? Urgency? What the hell could be so urgent? I'm a geologist for God's sake."

"Yes, sir," the agent replied. "We have our orders."

Branson dressed quickly and found himself whisked into the backseat of one of the vehicles. The car ride was exhilarating, to say the least. As sirens blared and tires screeched, Branson tightened his seatbelt. It wasn't until they exited the Baltimore-Washington Parkway onto Patuxent Freeway that he realized they were going to the headquarters of the National Security Agency.

"What are we doing here?" Branson said.

"Sorry, sir."

"I know, I know. You're not at liberty to say. Well, this one is for the books. A geologist is yanked out of bed at five in the morning to come to the NSA. Sure, happens all the time. Just another day for me."

"Yes, sir."

It took several minutes to negotiate the series of checkpoints. But once through the front doors and into the lobby of the sprawling NSA headquarters building, Branson tried to match pace with the speed-walking agents.

Uncle Bill stood just past the security checkpoint, wearing a crumpled, short-sleeve, button-down shirt; his hands clasped in front of him. As he extended a handshake, Branson took one look into his bloodshot eyes and knew this was a man that had not slept in a long time.

There was something about Bill's haggard, weary appearance that made Branson realize, whatever this was, it was big, maybe bigger than anything he'd been involved in before. And that was saying a lot.

Dr. Lyle Branson had signed on as a civilian contractor to the United States Navy a year and a half prior. At the time, the navy, under orders from Chief of Naval Operations Admiral Joseph Glass, had embarked on a project to map the ocean floor in the region of the Persian Gulf. For a geologist, it was the chance of a lifetime.

The United States and its allies needed oceanographic details of the area. As it happened, Branson had written his doctoral thesis on the technology surrounding high-resolution ultrasound images that could be used to document underwater geologic formations.

It sounded like such a great idea at the time. He would board the nuclear submarine, *USS Colorado*. From there he would be responsible for deploying ultrasound mapping equipment from the sub to create a detailed set of maps of the ocean floor in the region.

But the *Colorado* had stumbled upon a downed enemy submarine and the chaos began. By the time it was over, the *USS Colorado* had outmaneuvered a torpedo, destroyed another enemy sub, and narrowly escaped. It wasn't until later that Branson fully understood the naiveté of his agreement to do the project.

He was later astounded at himself. *What could go wrong?* he had thought. *What could go wrong is that you could end up dead, that's what could go wrong.*

Whatever the NSA wanted, Branson would certainly try to assist. But with his first experience with the federal government having gone so badly, he had hoped to never work for them again.

"Dr. Branson?" Uncle Bill said. "My name is William Tarleton. I'm sorry to have bounced you out of bed so early in the morning, but I need your help and it can't wait."

As the two made their way down the series of hallways to the command center, Bill made small talk, but Branson pressed for more.

"Mr. Tarleton, I still don't know why the NSA could possibly need a geologist."

"Oh, we'll get to that."

As they arrived at the command center, Bill put his hand on the door handle. "Dr. Branson, I can't emphasize enough the importance of what is happening here. What you are about to see and hear is highly classified. No one outside of this facility can know."

"I understand."

"I hope you do, sir. Word of this gets out on the street and we'll have an outright panic. Pandemonium in a way you've never seen. A lot of lives are on the line here, sir."

Bill slid his security card through the digital reader, but Branson put a hand on his arm. "Mr. Tarleton, are you sure you've got the right guy? Lives on the line? I'm a geologist. I study rock formations, underwater mountain ranges, tectonic plates, things like that. I don't know anything about national security."

"Tectonic plates, you say? Funny you should mention that." Bill pushed the door open.

"Well sure, lots of geologist have an interest in the study of tectonic plates, but why should that be of any interest to the NSA? Holy shit," Branson said. "This place is huge." His head craned in all directions as he studied the multiple large-screen computer monitors hanging from the ceiling.

Even at this hour of the morning, the place buzzed with activity. "Why the NSA's interest in tectonic plates? Did you run out of things to eavesdrop on?"

Bill gave him a blank stare.

"Sorry, geologist humor."

"Why don't you wait in here," Uncle Bill said as he pointed to the war room. "I'll bring you a cup of coffee. We'll get started in just a minute."

Knuckles walked in and rubbed his eyes as Uncle Bill peered across the tops of his glasses at him. "Just wake up? You look like you put your finger in an electrical socket."

"Oh, ah, yeah," he said as he attempted to comb his hair with his fingers.

"Put on a hat or something, son. We bounced Mr. Branson here out of bed at five and he looks like he'd be ready for a briefing with the president. Show some sense of decorum, will you?"

"Man, it's early. Besides, I gave away my NSA ball cap."

"Get Jana and the gang on the video uplink. They're at the FBI field office in San Fran," Uncle Bill said. "It's about two thirty in the morning there, but this can't wait."

By the time the secure video uplink connected, Branson paced the floor.

"Am I being detained?" Branson said.

"Detained?" Uncle Bill said. "No, but that sounds like something I ask my wife from time to time. Anytime my in-laws stay with us for the holidays, that is. No sir. But now that we're all gathered, I can tell you why I've asked you here."

"Asked me here? They dented my door just trying to wake me up."

"Everything we're about to tell you is classified, Dr. Branson. We need your help. I'll reiterate again. There is nothing we say that you can take outside of this room." Then he turned to the monitor and said, "Gang, this is Dr. Lyle Branson. He's a geologist and he's come here this morning out of the goodness of his heart."

"Goodness of my heart? Yeah, that's hysterical."

"This is a matter of national security, Dr. Branson. We do thank you for being here nonetheless."

"I'm not so sure I want to hear this," Branson said.

Bill continued. "Dr. Branson, joining us on secure video uplink are Special Agents Jana Baker and Kyle MacKerron. Cade Williams is one of my team. We're tracking another terrorist inside the United States." He let that statement hang in space for a moment. "We fear another nuclear attack."

Branson's head snapped in Bill's direction.

"A nuclear attack? And for some reason you need a geologist? Let me guess, you picked me because the nuclear device that destroyed CIA headquarters was obtained right out in front of the submarine USS Colorado when I was on board. Am I right?"

Bill saw no need to verify the information.

"What we're wondering is this," Bill said as he pointed to a map of the San Andreas Fault line.

"You want to ask me about the fault line?"

"Dr. Branson, is there any man-made way to trigger a major earthquake along the San Andreas Fault?"

Branson peered sideways at Bill. "This is just a wild guess, but you mean, as in placing a nuclear device inside the fault line?" He exhaled, then crossed his arms.

"I take it that this concept is not as far-fetched as it seems."

"Geologists have been squabbling about this for years. The consensus though, is that, yes, it's possible. But no one knows for sure. A lot of factors would have to be in place, and even if they were in place, it's still a long shot."

"Like what kind of factors?" Knuckles said.

"The fault line is made up of the Pacific plate and the North American plate. Those two plates are grinding against one another—one moving south, the other, north. The San Andreas Fault is called a right lateral transform fault. Sometimes a lot of tension builds up between the two plates, and finally, that tension gives way. That's when we get an earthquake. But right after the earthquake, the tension has settled out and is no longer present, at least for a while."

"And?" Uncle Bill pressed.

"One factor is that the plates would have to be under extreme tension, otherwise nothing would happen. And second, it would have to be an enormous device. The plates are like springs. The springs are hundreds of miles long and several miles thick. They weigh tens of thousands, or even trillions of tons. It would take a near-biblical force to move them."

Uncle Bill said, "Let's assume the plates are under great tension in the general vicinity of San Francisco. Well, hold on a second. Is there any way to know that they're under tension?"

"Well sure. The plates are continually moving and that is something we can feel and measure. When the plates touch each other they get stuck. The tension keeps pushing against the plates until finally enough stress is built up. Sometimes we detect more tectonic activity. But to answer your question, there's almost always a lot of tension across the plates."

"Do you believe?" Jana said. "Do you believe that it's possible a nuclear device could cause an earthquake?"

Branson's hands found their way into his pockets. "I tend to think it's a load of crap, personally."

"And why is that?" Jana said.

"We're talking about a fault line that stretches for *seven hundred miles*. Most of it is over ten miles deep, for God's sake. Like I said before. It would take a catastrophically large nuclear device to even make it budge."

"Like how large?" Bill said.

"Let me put it into perspective for you. The 1906 San Francisco earthquake was a 7.8 magnitude. And, no, that's not the largest one ever recorded in that region of the world. The largest was a 9.2 that happened in Alaska in 1964. But to give you an idea of the energy expended, the San Francisco earthquake of 1906 unleashed the energy equivalent of a forty-kiloton nuclear device. Bear in mind that the energy is spread across hundreds of miles. That's unlike what happens when a nuclear device detonates, where all the energy is delivered in one spot. During that particular earthquake, the earth shifted a full six meters. That's the very definition of devastation."

"*Forty* kilotons?" Jana said. She looked at Uncle Bill. "He's got that covered in spades."

"Who's got what covered in spades?" Branson said.

"She's talking about the terrorist, Dr. Branson," Bill said. "The device he has access to."

"It's bigger?"

Bill stood and began to walk out of the war room.

"Dr. Branson, the forty kiloton device you describe is roughly the size of the largest nuclear device ever tested. The device the terrorist has his hands on isn't measured in kilotons. It's measured in megatons. It's a ten megaton device. For comparison's sake, he doesn't have a forty kiloton device, he has a ten-thousand-kiloton device."

"Mother of God," Branson muttered as his eyes traced the floor.

"So what do you think now?" Jana asked. "Do you believe?"

"Ten thousand kilotons? If you could deliver ten thousand kilotons of energy into a focused point along the fault line . . . a bomb that large could set off a multimeter shift in the tectonic plates along hundreds of miles of the California landscape. The effect would be catastrophic."

Bill placed a hand on the door frame. "I want all of you to create a list of the most likely places to position the device along the fault line. Think like a terrorist and tell me where you'd place it, and why. And you should start your search at San Francisco."

33

THE MINE SHAFT

After Uncle Bill left the war room, the geologist, Branson, stood motionless. It was Jana who broke his fog.

"Dr. Branson," she said across the video monitor. "That seems so formal. Can we just call you Branson? Look, I know this is a bit of a shock—"

"A bit of a shock? I'm a geologist! I'm not used to this crap. Why in the hell I ever signed on board the *USS Colorado* last year is beyond me. If I hadn't done that, I wouldn't be sitting in NSA headquarters with the knowledge that a terrorist is out there, ready to detonate inside the United States again."

"I'm sorry," Jana said. "We unfortunately have gotten used to this. We're dealing with the same terrorist, the one who tried to detonate a nuclear device two years ago in Kentucky, and the one who *did* detonate a device last year at CIA headquarters. I think we're just numb to it now."

"You're numb to it? How could you be numb to it?" He looked at the three in turn. "Well un-numb yourselves, dammit."

"Yes, sir," Knuckles said. "Maybe we could just focus on your area of expertise."

"I'm sorry," Branson said as he slumped into a seat. "It's all just a bit overwhelming. Can we start over? I don't suppose there are any donuts around here to go with the stale coffee?"

Kyle laughed. "The stale coffee is an Uncle Bill specialty."

Knuckles continued. "What we need, Dr. Branson, is for you to think like a terrorist."

Branson's mouth hung open.

"If you were a terrorist and had this idea to place a nuclear device inside the fault line, where would you put it? Is there a place, or places, that would be particularly vulnerable? And remember, the terrorist would be looking for the place that would cause the most magnified effect possible."

Branson stood and began to pace. "Think like a terrorist, he says." He was almost talking to himself. "Think like a terrorist. Well, let's see, where would I place a bomb?" He looked at the monitor. "That's a good question. There isn't really a place along the fault line that would be considered more vulnerable in terms of how much pressure it's under. And even if there was, brilliant geologists like me can't really determine that. We don't have enough data." The grin on his face made him look as if he was waiting for a response. "That was geologist humor. Sorry."

Knuckles turned toward the glass wall and looked into the NSA control center. "There has to be a place Jarrah would choose. There's got to be something we're missing. Dr. Branson. We can't position surveillance units along seven hundred miles of California. It would take thousands of people. We have to narrow it down. We'll never be able to protect that big a strip of land." Knuckles was in his element now. "The clues we've been finding during this investigation have all pointed to this region up here," he said as he pointed to the map. "It's a strip of farmland used for producing fig trees, a particular species of fig tree, in fact. The details are not important, but this particular terrorist keeps pointing here. As you can see, these topographic maps and satellite views indicate a large swath of acreage dedicated to fig orchards. The reason we thought to consult you in the first place was because this entire orchard abuts the San Andreas Fault, all along this edge."

Branson removed his tweed sport coat and draped it over the back of a chair. "Consult with me? A bunch of FBI agents show up at my door at four-something in the morning and tell me to get dressed, then bring me here, and you call that consulting?"

Jana raised her hand. "That was my fault, Branson. The FBI agents, I mean. But please understand, we are under a lot of time pressure here. This isn't a case where we have any room for error. The terrorist has pulled off four assassinations as a buildup to this attack. At each of the murder scenes, he's left clues, and they all lead to this geography. We have further reason to believe that those are the only four murders he's going to pull off as he builds up to the detonation. What I'm saying is, we are out of time."

"Okay, okay, I'm sorry. Here I am getting pissed off that I've been dragged out of bed. That, and thinking about the fact that I'm supposed to give a lecture at Georgetown in about two hours. Oh well, those kids don't pay attention to my lectures anyway. So, where were we? All right, looking at your map, there's nothing unusual about this stretch of the San Andreas. A nuclear device placed anywhere along here would produce exactly the same result. And all of this land is a good distance away from the city of San Francisco itself. It's not as if the blast radius could impact the city if he detonated in this farmland." He looked at Knuckles. "A ten-megaton device wouldn't have that type of range, would it?"

Knuckles shook his head. "No, the blast radius would only cover between one and 1.1 miles of flat land. That's why we started wondering whether or not he could set off an earthquake which would damage the city that way."

"Well I don't think I'll be much help," Branson said. "He could set up the device anywhere along that region, and it would have the same impact on San Francisco. In my estimation, he could cause a substantial earthquake, but it's hard to say if it would have that much damage on the city."

Jana looked at him. "Well, let me ask you this. If you were a terrorist, and you had unlimited funds, and no one was watching, what would you do to make this the most effective strike on the city of San Francisco?"

"Hmmm," Branson said. "I suppose if I had enough time, I'd want to drill the deepest hole possible, directly into the fault line itself. That way I could place the device way down deep. All of the energy from the blast would be contained underground. It would be directly transferred into the two competing tectonic plates. A large enough device could cause quite a shift, which would unleash a massive earthquake." Branson nodded. "Yeah, that's what I'd do. I'd drill a great big hole—"

Jana said, "Branson? You kind of stopped midsentence there."

But he was entranced with his own thought. "A deep hole. That it!" He spun around to face the video monitor as his arms flew into the air. "I know where he's going to strike!"

34

TARGET ACQUIRED

"It's here!" Branson yelled, pointing to the map. "Right here, at Parkfield! Why didn't I think of that before?"

"What's Parkfield?" Knuckles said.

"It's the site of the drilling effort that began in 2004. The research observatory? Anybody following me?"

"No," Jana said.

"The San Andreas Fault is the site of a massive effort to drill into the earth's crust to investigate the fault at depth. It's the only place in the world anything like this has ever been attempted. And it's here at the town of Parkfield, California. The *San Andreas Fault Observatory at Depth*, or SAFOD, they call it. The hole is nearly two miles deep, drilled straight into the fault line."

"But Parkfield looks like it's over two hundred miles from San Francisco. How could he damage the city from that distance?" Knuckles said.

"Maybe it's not San Francisco he's after," Jana said.

Branson interrupted. "Whether or not the city of San Francisco is his primary objective, Parkfield is too perfect of a target not to hit. In geologist terms, it's a no-brainer. And, wait a

169

minute. A major earthquake in this region would be catastrophic to other areas as well. The more I think about it, San Francisco could be his target after all. Here, look at the map. Parkfield sits at the southern edge of the area of the fig plantations, right? And, there hasn't been a major earthquake in the region for close to twenty years. The tension along the fault line in this region is building."

"Like how much tension?" Knuckles said.

"Well, the fault line is divided into giant segments. The northern segment generally produces more powerful earthquakes. That's because those areas of the fault line are locked, meaning the rock is stuck against itself. When it finally lets loose the results are catastrophic. There hasn't been a major earthquake in that segment since the 1980s. Tension is enormous. But here, here at Parkfield, and stretching all the way up to the city of Hollister, that's what we call the *creeping* segment. As the name implies, the creeping segment moves more slowly. The earth in this region is made up of slippery clays, talc-like minerals that make for less dramatic earthquakes when the earth does shift. The two opposing sections of the fault line slip across one another without much violence. But it's these northern sections, the locked sections, that cause the worst damage."

"That doesn't make sense," Jana said. "Parkfield is in the creeping segment. You said the earthquakes there aren't as severe. So how is that going to cause an earthquake in San Fran?"

"Look, if you put a nuclear device down here in the creeping segment, the shock wave from the blast would radiate up the fault line with relative ease. When those shock waves hit the locked section of the fault line, the effect would magnify itself." Branson's mouth hung open. "*Catastrophic* might not be the word for it. I think the word might be closer to *apocalyptic.*"

Inside the FBI field office, Cade leaned closer to Jana and said, "Maybe *that's* the misdirection you were talking about. Maybe he wants us to think he'd hit the fault line as close to San Francisco as possible, when actually he intends to strike way down here at Parkfield."

Jana shook her head. "Misdirection."

Kyle walked toward her. "Well if we agree he's going to use it," he looked at the others, "you don't think he's going to use it here? Jana, come on. This is the perfect opportunity for him to inflict an incredible amount of damage up and down California. The nutjob probably thinks he's going to cause half of California to slump off into the ocean."

"Which is crap," Branson said.

Jana stood. "What's there? At Parkfield? How big of a town is it? What kind of facilities are we talking about?"

"At Parkfield itself? Well there's not much there. I've never been myself, but it looks like a big oil-drilling rig. I don't think there's much there in terms of buildings, but I'm sure there's a few laboratories. The town isn't actually a town at all, more like a crossroads and maybe a red light."

"No security?" Jana said.

"Security?" Branson said. "Security in case some nutjob decides he wants to drop a nuclear device down a mine shaft? Sorry, that's not likely one of the things the US Geological Survey would have considered."

"Wait a minute," Kyle said. "I've been listening to this whole thing. There's one part that doesn't make any sense. Even if Jarrah wanted his device to detonate at the bottom of the mine shaft, how's he going to get it down there? If this mine shaft looks like an oil-drilling rig, then the rig has a giant drillbit running all the way down the shaft. There wouldn't be any room to drop an object of this size down it."

"Good point," Knuckles said. "With the massive drill auger in place, I don't think anything over a few inches wide could slip past."

Branson's face washed clear of color and he slumped into a chair.

"Branson?" Jana said.

He looked at each person. "How would he be able to get the device to the bottom of the mine shaft, you ask? Drilling operations stopped sometime back. I think it was last January. The drill auger and the entire drilling rig were disassembled. We're talking about a two-foot wide hole, two miles deep, straight to the base of the fault line itself. He would just drop it in."

35

OVEREXPOSED

"Knuckles," Jana said, "pull up satellite imagery on Parkfield. Let's take a look at what's there. This is a small town, right? My question is, how is he going to hide in a small town like that? And what is his plan, to walk right up to the mine shaft and dump a nuclear device down it? I don't buy it. It's too obvious."

"Bring it up, son," Uncle Bill said.

"Yes, sir. Here it is on satellite. Let me zoom this closer."

"Just like I thought," Jana said. "Look at the surrounding area. It's not even a town. There's only a couple of buildings. How old is this satellite imagery? A few months? And look, it's like Branson said, they disassembled the drilling rig. There's almost nothing there but a chain-link fence to keep someone from falling into the mine shaft."

"Maybe it is that simple," Cade said.

"Sure, it would be easy to walk right up and get past that fence," Jana continued. "But he'd be out in the open, exposed. I can't see him tipping his hand this far to point us right to the spot. He would know we would be waiting for him. I still say something is wrong."

Bill stood and his shoulders pulled back. "Jana, I hear what you're saying, but we can't take any chances. I want the three of you down there. I'll get on the phone with Washington. We're sending at least one hostage-rescue team to the scene. Jana, Kyle, Cade? You hear me? I want you at the airport right now. Get to Parkfield. We don't have any time to waste."

Kyle said, "Bill, I think we need to talk."

Uncle Bill knew Kyle believed Jana's PTSD made her a liability in the field. It was the proverbial "elephant in the room."

"That's a negative, Agent MacKerron."

"Sir, I've got to reiterate—"

"Enough. Your comment is duly noted."

Kyle exhaled. "Yes, sir. But, Bill? When you talk to Washington, remember, we've got to keep a low profile. If Jarrah sees a bunch of badass operators with automatic weaponry and body armor, it might kind of tip our hand. Know what I mean? Hostage Rescue Team needs to know this is a plain-clothes scenario. We all need to blend in."

"Wait," Jana said. "Kyle, what was that all about?"

Uncle Bill quickly diverted. "Yeah, you'll need civilian clothes and vehicles."

Knuckles looked up at him. "Hey, maybe they should use your new minivan."

"New minivan?" Cade said.

Uncle Bill cocked his head at Knuckles. "They won't be taking that minivan. The NSA has never replaced the first one of my wife's vans that was destroyed. I still can't find a spot on the expense report form with enough zeros to write off a Honda Odyssey."

After the others left the room, Cade turned to Jana. "I know you are not buying this, Jana. But this is the most likely scenario."

"What was Kyle talking about?"

"Come on, we need to get to the flight line."

Jana shook her head at him, knowing he had purposely not answered her question. "He's not going to be there, Cade. Jarrah is sending us on another goose chase, just like he did last time when we followed the trail of nuclear material that led to nowhere. I'm inside his head. I know this is misdirection."

"We'll talk about it on the plane. We need to find the nearest airport to Parkfield. There's sure as hell no landing strip in that little place. And one more thing."

"Yeah?"

"Did Uncle Bill just send me to the field again? Dammit, he's going to have to stop doing that."

36

HANDSHAKE OF REGRET

San Francisco International Airport, en route to Parkfield, California

The Gulfstream rocketed down San Francisco International Airport's runway 19L, an 8,600-foot-long strip of pale concrete. Jana, Cade, and Kyle pulled their seat belts tight.

Kyle looked at Jana and shook his head. "I can see it in your face, Jana. I know what you're thinking. And sure, I understand you don't believe Parkfield is his target. But I'll ask again. If we don't go to Parkfield to follow up on this, where else are we going to go?"

"Yeah, Jana," Cade said. "We've got a hundred and sixty agents scouring the downtown San Francisco area, looking for anything that might be trouble."

"Not to mention the radiation sensors being flown in as we speak. They'll have them positioned in the next two hours."

"I know, I get it. But I still say San Francisco is not his target. And that means Parkfield is not his target either."

Cade said, "Why not Parkfield?"

"Parkfield is just a means to an end. In theory, if he detonates at Parkfield the shock wave will cause utter destruction in San Francisco. But like I said, San Fran is not his target."

"Dammit, Jana," Kyle said. "We have nothing else to go on. This is not only the best lead we have, it makes absolute sense. We're going to find him, and find him at Parkfield."

Jana's eyes drifted out the window. "Well, if you're right, and we do find him, I'm going to kill him on sight."

"Jana," Cade lashed, "I told you before, I don't want to hear talk like that. You're not a murderer."

"Well maybe I should be. I appreciate your desire to do things by the book, but tell that to the eight hundred thousand Americans who were vaporized in Virginia last year."

"That's not fair, and you know it."

"Let's change the subject," Kyle said. "The flight to Parkfield's nearest airport is only about forty-five minutes. The pilot said he's going to get us as close to the town as possible. Obviously, there's no airport in Parkfield."

Cade said, "Not even an airstrip?"

"Apparently not. In fact, the airports in the surrounding area are tiny. It took the pilot a minute to find one with an adequate runway for landing. He said no worries though. He found one about twenty-five miles southwest of the town. It's a place called McMillan Field. Small, but it will do."

"I assume we have FBI to meet us there?" Cade said. "You know, it might kind of help if we had a car on the ground when we get there."

"Yeah, no kidding. Way ahead of you, pal," Kyle replied. "I put Knuckles on the job. Hey, Jana, listen, we're going to get him this time. Are you with me?"

But Jana's fingers found their way to her sternum where they rubbed a bullet-hole scar. Her gaze seemed locked as if she was awake, but seeing nothing.

"Jana?" Cade said. "Stay with us, okay?"

Jana's eyes did not shift. "Oh, I'm still with you. Just a little preoccupied at the moment."

Cade said, "Try not to focus on that right now." As a means of distracting her from the memory of the shooting incident that left her near dead, he added, "What will be the first thing we do when we get to the ground?"

"Well, we all get in a bureau car and drive to the middle of nowhere. There we'll sit on stakeout and find nothing." She closed her eyes. "Unless we figure something else out, we're going to be looking at another spot in the United States that has been vaporized."

The secure-video-conference line blinked to life and the three found Knuckles staring into the camera.

"Hey guys," Knuckles said as he tapped his fingers on the video camera. "Mind turning on your camera? I can't see anything."

"So impatient." Cade flipped on the power switch and said, "That better?"

"Hey, listen. I tried, but I can't find an asset anywhere in the area to meet you guys on the ground."

Jana spoke up in sudden escalation, "What? We can't just be sitting at an airport doing nothing."

"I know, I know. So I got the US Geological Survey office to lend you a car. You might be sitting for a little while until it arrives. Best I could do."

Kyle laughed. "You procured a vehicle from the US Geological Survey? How appropriate."

"I thought so," Knuckles said. "They were a little startled when I called, but since they're US government as well, I convinced them to cut through the red tape and just loan you a vehicle for a while. Probably some beat-up pickup truck though."

"Whatever," Jana said. "We're wasting our time anyway."

It was fifteen minutes later when the plane touched down at McMillan Field.

"Wow, not much here," Jana said.

But as the plane taxied to a halt, she looked out at an approaching vehicle. "That doesn't look like a rusty pickup truck. That's bureau."

Kyle said, "I guess Knuckles did better at finding us an available asset than he thought. Good, we could use the help. And yes, Jana, we're going to need help, because *this* is the location. It may take a while, but we'll find Jarrah in Parkfield."

The pilot opened the plane's door and dropped the staircase to the ground. Jana, followed by Cade, then Kyle, disembarked.

A man exited the black Chevy Suburban and held out FBI credentials.

"Special Agent Baker," Jana said as she extended the man a firm handshake. "This is MacKerron and Williams."

He looked at them through steely-eyed Ray Bans. "Ramirez, bureau. Right this way. Parkfield is only twenty-five miles from here. I only had a short briefing, so you'll have to fill me in on the way. Do you want lights and siren or do we need to go in without drawing attention?"

As the group boarded the vehicle Jana instinctively took the front passenger seat. It was her command and she wanted anyone on-site with them at Parkfield to know it.

She said, "Just so you know, Ramirez, whatever assignment they pulled you off was more important than this one."

"Jana," Cade said, "would you drop it already? There isn't a more important assignment anywhere in the bureau right now. Ramirez, is it? We need to keep this low profile. We'll have at least one HRT group here within two hours. But until then, we're on our own. We need to get into the town and get somewhere we can surveil the mine shaft without being noticed."

As he pulled the vehicle away, Ramirez started to cough.

"You okay?" Jana said. "You're not going to keel over on us, are you?"

Through repeated coughs, Ramirez said, "No, I'm fine. Allergies. As soon as I got reassigned out here, they flared up something awful. In fact, I have to go on filtered air sometimes. I feel like an idiot when I put this thing on, but," he shrugged, "doctor's orders." He affixed a nasal cannula with mask over his nose and mouth. The clear translucent mask had an oxygen tube running to it. His coughing intensified.

"Man, never seen allergies that bad," Kyle said. "I wouldn't have thought allergies would be bad out here in the arid country."

Ramirez reached down and turned the handle on what appeared to be a small oxygen container stowed in front of him. It let out a loud hiss.

"God, Ramirez. That stuff stinks. What the hell are you breathing in anyway?" But by the time Jana completed her sentence, her vision began to blur and her head slumped against the door. Then, everything went black.

37

LEVEL C

Emergency Room, Stanford Hospital, Templeton, California

The emergency room erupted into organized chaos. "All right everybody, listen up!" Dr. Adele Lindquist yelled to the staff of medical personnel as they scrambled into positions.

"We are *level C*, yellow zone. Under advisement from the National Institute for Occupational Safety and Health, we will follow the acute exposure guidelines to the letter. In the remaining thirty seconds we have before the ambulances arrive, here's a refresher so you don't screw it up. These are sets of short-term exposure limits for acutely toxic chemicals. Every one of you need to strap on your NIOSH-certified air-purifying respirator right now. No one removes their chemical resistant suit until we give the all clear. That means chemical-resistant gloves, boots, face shield, disposable boot covers, I want it all."

"What have we got?" a male doctor with salt-and-pepper hair yelled as he ran into the emergency room. When he saw the biohazard suits, his eyes widened with fear.

"Inbound at this time, two males, each approximately thirty years of age, one, a hundred and sixty, the other, a hundred and eighty pounds. Both suffering from acute exposure to what we believe to be an aerosolized form of 3-methylfentanyl."

A male nurse pulled tightly against rubber gloves and said, "How do we know they've been exposed to fentanyl?"

"We've got two ambulance drivers, also down. Both were overcome with the fumes when they arrived on scene. When the fire crew arrived, they donned oxygen masks to extract the victims from the vehicle. Inside was a canister labeled *3-methylfentanyl*. It's pretty clear." Her volume escalated. "This is not a drill, people. This is the real thing. We're breaking up into two teams. Each team will handle one victim. The two ambulance drivers that were overcome with fumes have been diverted to Atascadero State Hospital. But the two coming here are far more critical. We don't know how long they've been exposed, nor what dose they received."

The faint sound of a pair of sirens began a slow increase in volume as two ambulances neared the emergency-room entrance.

"Get your patient to the wash station. Put them in a standing position and cut the clothes away, then start an aggressive wash with the soap-and-water solution before you transfer them to the gurney. Brush the toxins off the skin. Make sure you move from the head to the toe. Fentanyl is a potent opioid, approximately one hundred times more potent than morphine. Check for signs of respiratory depression, low oxygen saturations, pinpoint pupils with subsequent bradycardia and hypotension. There may be some chest wall rigidity. Spasms are common. Hypoxia, acidosis, check the heart for bradycardia, shock. Expect a slowing in gastric hypomotility characterized by hypoactive bowel sounds when auscultating the abdomen. Treatment regimen is as follows. First, get those airways clear! Mechanical ventilation as needed. We'll start Narcan, 0.4 milligrams, but ramp it up to two milligrams immediately if you're not seeing a response."

The ambulance bay doors burst open and two teams dressed in hazmat suits pushed gurneys through. Special Agent Kyle MacKarren lay on one and Cade Williams on the other. Both men were unconscious.

"Move, people, move!" the doctor yelled.

38

HEAT SIGNATURE

NSA Command Center

"Uncle Bill!" Knuckles yelled. "They found them!"

"My God. Are they all right? Where are they?"

They were found halfway between the airport and the town of Parkfield. Both are unconscious. They're being transported to the emergency room now."

"What you mean, *both* of them?"

"That's just it, sir. They found Agent MacKerron and Cade, but they haven't found Jana yet."

Uncle Bill gripped each side of his head. "Jana is missing? What the hell happened? We lose contact with them for eight hours, and now you're telling me Jana is missing?"

"Yes, sir. I just reverified it with Special Agent Philip Murphy, leader of hostage-rescue team two. They were on-site at Parkfield. They've been scouring the hills for hours. It was the Monterey County Sheriff's Department helicopter that found them. It picked up a heat signature using thermal-imaging equipment on board. Kyle and Cade were found inside a vehicle that had been parked in an old shed up in the hillsides. It's a miracle they were located. Agent Murphy is on-site at the shed now, but he can't get too close to the vehicle. The whole scene is a hazmat disaster. Some kind of toxin must've been used to knock them unconscious."

Bill stared at the boy. "They were rendered unconscious? Jana, my God. Jana. She's been kidnapped." Bill began to pace the floor, entranced in his own thoughts. "This is my fault . . . oh God, this is my fault. I could have pulled her off the active list . . . I could have . . . eight hours, eight hours. For all we know, she was abducted and has been removed from the area. She could be anywhere by now. And . . . what if they are . . .," his volume descended to a whisper, "hurting her? I'll never forgive myself." He drew in a deep breath and blew it out, then arched his chest and scanned the room. "People, we're going to find Agent Baker. Drop everything you're doing. Use your override codes to retask the nearest available satellites to sweep the area."

"Uncle Bill?" Knuckles said. "Drop everything we're doing? I know this is Jana we're talking about. I love her too. But our first priority has to stay tracking the nuclear weapon."

"I know that, son. But it's my belief that tracking Agent Jana Baker will lead us right to the bomb. You're going to have my job one day, son, and you will be welcome to it." Bill put his hands on his hips. "Damn, times like this I really miss Stevie Latent. Get on the horn to the FBI. We need all the hostage-rescue team operators they can send. And tell them not to bother trying to keep a low profile. I want that countryside swarming with Kevlar."

39

GROTESQUE

State Route 14, Crystal Springs, Nevada, approximately 493 miles west of Parkfield, California

As Jana regained consciousness, she found herself in a world of pain. Everything burned, her throat, lungs, eyes, and much of her skin. Drawing in air was painful. Her chest felt like it was made out of wood. Her vision blurred and she felt a pain in her left hand as if she was being jabbed by something sharp. As she tried to recoil against it, she found her hands cuffed behind her back.

Rafael laughed. "Starting to wake up, I see. That's more than I can say for your two friends. I doubt they will ever wake up again. You have me to thank, you know. I pulled you out of that vehicle as soon as you were unconscious. You didn't get exposed to a fraction of what your friends did."

Jana's vision began to clear, but everything looked hazy around the edges. She tried to speak but couldn't.

"That was another injection of Narcan I just gave you. That is your third. Exposure to toxic levels of fentanyl are often fatal, Miss Baker. Narcan has to be administered multiple times to counteract the effects."

Rafael started the engine of the white van and pulled into the inky darkness of the rural highway.

Jana muscled herself into a more upright, seated position, then looked out the side window. She found it tinted so darkly, she could see nothing. This time as she tried to speak, a few sounds emerged, although nothing distinguishable.

"Oh, Miss Baker. Do not try to speak. You Americans always have too much to say. And after a second nuclear device detonates on this land of yours, many more of you will be silenced. But none of that is of interest to me. I work at the pleasure of those who employ my services. I am good at what I do, yes. But what I do, I do for the money. It is as simple as that."

He glanced at Jana and his eyes ran across her body, drinking in the feminine shape.

"I have been given specific instructions with you, Miss Baker. As I'm sure you have surmised, my employer is your dear friend, Waseem Jarrah. He knows me well enough to know I have specific tastes in women. His eyes again ran across her body.

Jana leaned away from him, against the passenger door. But even small movement proved difficult. To Jana, her body felt as if she were almost paralyzed.

"And lucky for you, he forbade me from violating you just yet. Although now that I sit next to you, I regret accepting that condition. Many of the women in my past have not been so lucky."

Rafael leaned toward Jana and placed his hand inside her button-down shirt. She tried to pull away but couldn't. Her breathing accelerated and her anger exploded, but there was nothing she could do as his hand found its way underneath her bra. The grotesque act stopped as quickly as it had started.

"Very nice. There will be time for that later though. Once

Jarrah is finished with you, you are mine."

Jana's consciousness began to fade and her head slumped against the passenger-door window with a heavy thud.

40

MAGMA

"Try not to talk, man," Kyle said as he leaned over Cade's hospital bed. "There's a breathing tube inserted in your throat. Don't worry, they're going to take it out in a minute. They say you're going to be fine. They say we're both going to be fine. But no one is telling me anything. I just woke up about thirty minutes ago myself. I don't know about you, but I feel like a freight train ran over me. Everything hurts."

Cade squeezed his eyes shut, then opened them again, trying to focus on the room.

"We're in a hospital. I don't remember anything either. And no, I have no idea how we got here."

Dr. Lindquist walked in. "Good, you're awake. Let's get that tube out of your throat, shall we?"

She walked to the other side of the bed and tightened the band holding her long brunette hair in a ponytail. "Now, Mr. Williams, on the count of three I'm going to remove the tube. When I say three I want you to cough, and cough loudly, okay?"

As the tube was extricated from Cade's throat, he coughed until nearly gagging.

189

"Try not to talk right away," Dr. Lindquist said. "Give it a minute." She looked at the two men. "But now that I have the two of you together, let me tell you what's going on. You've been exposed to a chemical called 3-methylfentanyl."

Kyle's voice sounded like a parched desert. "3-methyl-what? How did we get exposed to some chemical? Everything is so hazy in my memory."

"That's not for me to determine," she said. "However it happened, this kind of exposure is incredibly rare, and often times, fatal. Some derivative of this same chemical was used by Russian special forces during the Moscow theater hostage crisis back in 2002. One hundred and thirty people died due to the exposure, and lack of medical treatment to revive them. It's one of the most potent sedation agents in the world. The two of you are lucky to be alive."

Cade's eyes stared, half-open, as he looked at the doctor. "The two of us?" he whispered. "What do you mean, the two of us? Where's Jana? Where's Agent Baker?" He turned to Kyle. "Kyle, don't tell me she's dead."

"Cade, I keep asking the same question. Nobody is talking."

From out in the hallway a slight altercation erupted.

"Well, I need to get in there!" a man yelled.

A nurse replied, "Listen here. I don't know what your mother taught you, but this is the intensive care unit and we don't care who you are."

"Good lord. A man spends the better part of his adult life getting shot at in the line of duty and he can't even get in to see one of his agents. Do you know how high my top-secret security clearance runs? Well, it's pretty high. Not that it will cut any slack around here."

Kyle put a hand behind himself to close the flaps on his hospital gown, then shuffled into the hall. Even in the tension of their situation, Kyle had to laugh at what he saw next.

"Ouch!" Commander Murphy said. "That hurts!" He turned to Kyle. "Did you see that? She pinched my ear! Dang, lady. That's just mean."

The nurse smiled at him. "Well that's what you get when you try to break the rules. Didn't your mother ever teach you that?"

Kyle said, "He's okay, ma'am. Don't pay him any mind."

"My mama taught me plenty."

Agent Murphy walked into Cade's room with Kyle. "Man, she's mean." He looked back out in the hallway and found the nurse still smirking at him. "I'm not sure I'm mad at her, or if I like her. MacKerron, you feeling better? Damn, son, we thought we lost you. You too, Mr. Williams. Glad to see both of you alive and well."

"Sir," Kyle said. "What's going on? Where's Agent Baker?"

"That's the problem, son. We don't know. After your plane touched down, you three were out of contact for over eight hours. The only thing we knew was that the pilot said you disembarked the plane and got in a black Chevy Suburban. After that, it was like you were on the dark side of the moon. What's the last thing you remember?"

"We were picked up by a man identifying himself as a special agent, bureau. His name was Ramirez. Flashed his credentials. We didn't think anything of it. Just figured he'd been assigned to assist us on-site here. The rest gets a little hazy."

Cade sat up on his elbows and began to speak in a voice that sounded like he had pebbles in his throat.

"The guy started coughing as we were driving away, but I think it was all an act. Said something about his allergies flaring up. He put a mask on his face with an oxygen tube and started to breathe through it. That's when I heard a loud hissing sound. I assume that's when he released the knockout gas into the vehicle. Everything went black. Next thing I knew, I woke up here. But we're wasting time. We've got to find her."

"Sit tight, son. Don't try to get up. We've got one hundred seventy-five assets scouring the hillsides. I've got six helicopters and twelve canine units. I've got over three hundred civilian volunteers who have been hiking a grid pattern for the last four hours. But so far, we haven't found a thing."

Dr. Lindquist said, "Mr. Williams, I'm going to add another dose of Narcan to your IV unit. This should be your last one. You'll feel better shortly. But you need to sit back and rest."

"There's no way I'm staying here," Cade said as he began to push himself upright. "I've got to find her."

Dr. Lindquist grabbed him by the shoulders. "You're not leaving this hospital today. Doctor's orders. Just let them do their work. They'll find her."

But Cade and Kyle knew neither one could relax with Jana missing.

Kyle said, "They've really found nothing? How about witnesses?"

"Nothing. This is remote California hill country. We haven't found a single witness who could give us anything of value."

"He could've had another car stashed somewhere," Cade said. "He could have driven her out of the area by now." His voice skipped as his throat tightened. "We weren't found for eight hours, you said? And I've been unconscious for how long? Another eight? My God, they could be anywhere by now. We've got to find her!"

Cade again began to sit upright but Kyle held him back.

"Hold on, man. Even if we were both able to walk out of this place, we don't have any idea where we'd go."

Agent Murphy said, "Believe me, Mr. Williams, we've been on it. Every law enforcement department and agency in the region has been put on full alert. But at this point, we have nothing. We'll take your description of this Ramirez subject and put out an APB. I've got a secure uplink to NSA getting set up in here. In fact, I think I can hear my agents being scolded by that nurse. Ah, doctor, would you come out there with me to calm her down? We've got business to attend to."

"Certainly," Dr. Lindquist said as she departed the room.

As Agent Murphy turned to leave, Kyle said, "Not afraid of a little nurse, are you, Agent Murphy?"

"Not funny, MacKerron."

Within a few minutes a secure-satellite-uplink communications device was operational and Knuckles's face appeared on the monitor.

"Kyle? Cade? Thank God. You people scared me."

"Yes," Uncle Bill said as he walked into view. "I've said it before and I'll say it again. I'm getting too old for this shit."

"Bill," Cade said, "what have we got on Jana? Is there any way to find her?"

"Cade, we're analyzing satellite data from the two birds we were able to retask to the area. So far, we've got nothing. Even the exact location of where you and Kyle were found, in that old barn, is so obscured by trees, we can't even see the dirt path that leads to it."

"The target is not Parkfield, Bill."

"I'm beginning to agree with you," he replied. "At this point, we have to assume Parkfield was just a decoy. The team and I are thinking Jarrah set up all those clues to point us there for the sole purpose of diverting us and kidnapping Jana. Whether or not he knew he'd be able to pull off the kidnapping is anyone's guess. But even if that part of his plan never happened, Jarrah would still have succeeded in diverting our attention away from his actual detonation site."

"Which is where?" Kyle said.

Bill looked down and rubbed his neck. "Been working on that."

Cade's volume escalated. "Find the site and we find Jana."

Bill's head snapped back to the video monitor. "That's exactly what I've been saying. It would make perfect sense. Since we know it wasn't Jarrah himself that kidnapped her, the kidnapper, this Ramirez person, would likely be taking Jana to Jarrah. And Jarrah is almost certainly at or nearby the site where he intends to detonate."

"God, Bill," Cade said. "What if they're hurting her? What if . . . what if they're doing bad things to her?"

"I know, Cade, I know. I'm trying not to think about it. We've got to stay on point. We've got to figure out the actual target."

Knuckles said, "But, Uncle Bill, in his previous two attacks, Jarrah didn't intend to detonate the weapon himself. He always had one of his psycho jihadist followers do that."

"I know, son. But this time it all feels different." Bill's fingers descended into his beard. "In previous attacks, he hadn't yet been able to carry out his life's work—to detonate a nuke inside the US. Now that he's been successful, we all agree, he's having fun with this one. Remember, this is the last nuclear weapon in his possession. He obviously has a hired gun working with him on this, but I wouldn't doubt if he is ready and willing to do the deed himself this last time. Even if it means dying in the process. I don't think he cares anymore."

"So the question remains," Cade said. "If we agree Jana is being taken to Jarrah, then *where is Jarrah?*" Cade swallowed in an attempt to clear the lump forming in his throat. "If Jana is with him, she's going to be killed in the blast. Or, he's going to . . ." He couldn't continue.

"Don't think like that, man," Kyle said. "Hey, we're going to find her." He looked at the video monitor. "Bill, we have a list of all possible scenarios, right? At the top of the list is an attack on Washington, DC. Last year, that was the first place we thought of, and we were almost right. If he's headed that way—"

Bill cut him off. "Way ahead of you, Kyle. Washington is on lockdown."

"What do you mean?"

"It's a full-scale evacuation of the city. The order came down from the Director of National Intelligence himself. The National Counterterrorism Center has issued orders for the evacuation of all nonessential personnel, and for barricades to be erected. They're establishing a military perimeter around the city. Nothing will be allowed in that hasn't been swept with radiation-detection equipment."

"Jarrah might be able to drive up to a checkpoint," Knuckles said, "but he'd have to detonate right there. He'd cause terrible destruction, but he wouldn't be able to get close enough to take out the government."

"In fact," Uncle Bill said, "the president and joint chiefs have already been evacuated. The vice president is staying in residence, but most members of Congress are being moved as well. He can try, but he'll never get close enough."

"It's just like that passage in the book of Revelations," Kyle said, before he quoted, "'Then the kings of the earth and the great ones and the generals and the rich and the powerful, and everyone, hid themselves in the caves and among the rocks of the mountains.'" He shook his head. "Jarrah is winning. He's got us hiding. He's got our leaders hiding."

"I feel like shit," Cade said. "So, what do we do? We have to have a plan. We have to . . ." Then Cade squinted into the monitor.

"You okay, Cade?" Bill said.

"Is that Branson behind you?"

Uncle Bill turned to look at the man. "What about him? We already determined Jarrah isn't going to attack the San Andreas Fault—"

"I know, Bill," Cade said, this time launching out of the hospital bed and onto his feet. "Jarrah spent a lot of time diverting us to the fault line. But what about anything else geological? Remember what Jana said? She said during one of the phone calls, Jarrah stated he'd strike the place that would cause *more damage than anywhere else in the land.* What if Jarrah does have some kind of geological target in mind, and that's what got him thinking about diverting us to another? What if he was referring to anywhere in the United States, and not just California?"

"Hey Branson, mind giving us a hand over here?"

"Giving you a hand? Do I have a choice?"

"No," Bill replied.

"Didn't think so," Branson said as he walked closer into view of the video monitor. "Anything I can do for you? Any other information you want to share with me that's going to make me not be able to sleep ever again?"

"Sleep?" Uncle Bill said. "Who needs sleep? I haven't had any of that for about forty-eight hours. Cade has a question about other potential targets."

"Like what?"

"Anything. In your experience, is there any geological target in the US, outside of the San Andreas, that is, that would cause more destruction than anywhere else?"

"Other targets? Listen, you're talking to the wrong guy. I spent most of my career as a professor. I teach the stuff. You guys need a researcher. You know, someone who's spent their life in the field?"

"Dr. Branson," Bill said, "Not your entire career has been spent teaching. You went into the field for quite a research mission, I would say."

"Yeah," Knuckles said, "you took that tour of duty on the *USS Colorado*, surveying the ocean floor in the Persian Gulf."

"Don't remind me. I still have nightmares." Branson removed his tweed jacket and draped it over a chair. "I spent most of my career teaching oceanographic geology. You know, *wet dirt*. You guys need an expert in dry dirt."

"Branson," Cade said, "there's no easy way to say this so I'm going to say it. Jana's life is on the line. Lots of lives are on the line. Think, dammit, think."

"I'm thinking, all right? So, you guys want to know another geological target that a nuke could be used that would cause more destruction than the bomb itself. A magnified effect. And it's not the fault line? Hell, I was pretty proud of coming up with that one."

"Sorry to disappoint you," Uncle Bill said.

"Another target? Well, I suppose it would be effective to set one off inside an active volcano, if there were one. If an active volcano were nearing eruption, perhaps you'd get a combined effect. Yeah, that would work."

Bill crossed his arms. "But it would have to be active or getting close to active?"

"Correct. If the magma were nearing the surface, a nuclear detonation would be able to unleash the majority of the force of the eruption all at once."

"And what could that do?" Knuckles said.

"When a volcano erupts, even if it blows its top completely off, it's pretty rare that it blots out the sky, like is mentioned in the passages from the book of Revelations. It's more typical for it to explode and release the molten magma slowly."

"Mount Saint Helens didn't do that," Uncle Bill said. "I'm plenty old enough to remember that eruption."

"May 18, 1980," Branson said. "The explosion alone scorched an area two hundred and thirty square miles across. Ash rose to an altitude of eighty thousand feet. And the top of the mountain was reduced in altitude by thirteen hundred feet. It literally blew its top off. But we knew that one was building up. There's nothing like that happening in the US right now. Remember, the magma has to be close enough to the surface to be released, and the pressure buildup would have to be unbelievable. Otherwise, a nuclear detonation would probably just suppress any volcanic activity, not magnify it."

Cade steadied himself against Kyle. His balance and strength were returning. "And there's nothing like that happening now?"

"No."

"When's the last time something like that happened in the US? Something huge, besides Mount Saint Helens, I mean?"

"Oh, good God. Now you're talking about looking back six hundred and forty thousand years."

"Where did that one go off?" Bill said.

As if in slow motion, Branson bit his lower lip and turned his back to them.

"Branson?" Bill said. "What is it?"

41

TO BLACKEN THE SKY

NSA Command Center

"How could I have been so stupid?" Branson yelled, but then began to walk away as he continued talking to himself. "But I don't study this kind of thing. I barely pay any attention to it. It's the stuff of doomsdayers," he said as his arms flailed into the air. "That's not real science. That's for those guys that just want to get their names splashed across the news, scaring people half to death."

"Branson?" Bill said. "Hey, you still with us? We're over here."

"Oh, sorry. I just have a hard time with thrill-seekers in the geology world."

Cade erupted. "Spit it out! Branson, whatever you're thinking, get it on the table."

"It's the *caldera*. I can't believe I never thought about it before. But you guys were so busy getting me to think about California and the fault line. I never really considered anything else."

"What caldera?" Bill said.

"Jellystone," Branson said, hoping to elicit a laugh. "Uh, sorry. Yellowstone. The Yellowstone caldera."

"Tell us about it," Bill said. "And don't assume we know our

199

calderas from our references to *The Flintstones*."

"Yes, sir. A caldera is a huge impression or crater left behind when an old volcano collapses. Come to think of it, I'm surprised you don't know about it. If you guys spend as much time thinking up doomsday scenarios as I think you do, this one should be on your radar. Anyone following me? No? I'm talking about the Russian analyst that splashed himself across the news in March of 2015 by calling for a nuclear attack on the Yellowstone caldera itself. Most people thought he was nuts."

"And *is* he nuts?" Knuckles said, probing Branson to go deeper.

"Look, we've always known there was an ancient volcano under Yellowstone. Like I said, been dormant for six hundred and forty thousand years. But we didn't learn until 2013 that the magma chamber was so large. Enormous, in fact. But now that we know, the Yellowstone caldera is listed as one of the largest active continental volcanic fields in the world. When I said that Russian analyst was nuts, I meant that he was believed to be nuts because it was just so much political rhetoric. He's apparently the kind of guy who thinks Russia should take out the US in one swift stroke. But the science is real. The scientific community agrees that a full-scale eruption of the caldera would devastate the United States."

Bill looked over the tops of his glasses. "And how do you define 'devastate'?"

"Let's be clear here. We're talking about an eruption that no one feels is eminent. In fact, I think they estimated the probability of eruption on any given day to be something like one chance out of 700,000. But if it *were* to erupt, it would be one thousand times more powerful than the Mount Saint Helens blast. It would blacken the skies over much of the country. So much ash would fall, it would cause a yearlong winter. The US

Geological Survey predicts there would be molten ash ten feet thick for a thousand miles in any direction. Temperatures would drop, for God's sake." Branson was speaking fast enough to begin losing his breath. "Air travel would stop, people wouldn't be able to drive their cars. And think about how heavy ten feet of ash would be. Roofs would collapse, bridges, buildings—" He drew in a deep breath.

"He's right," Knuckles said, interrupting Branson. "Remember that eruption in Iceland in 2010? It stopped all air travel."

"Compared to this, that eruption would look like child's play. There would be a worldwide food shortage."

"Wait, wait," Kyle said. "You said the ash and damage would extend in any direction. Yellowstone is out in Montana, right?"

"Wyoming."

"So how would western areas in the US be affected by that? The jet stream blows everything east."

Branson's arms again flew into the air. "You're not getting it! This thing would be so huge *it would create its own wind*. It would disrupt the entire jet stream. There would be two inches of ash in New York City." His chest heaved. "Oh my God. I don't feel so good. I think I'm going to be sick."

Knuckles grabbed him around the waist and guided him into a chair.

"Here, sit down. Hey, Mr. Branson."

Branson looked at him through bloodshot eyes. "Aren't you, like, fifteen years old? That's Doctor Branson to you."

"Yes, sir. Listen, it's going to be okay, okay?"

"That certainly makes me feel better," Branson said as he tried to laugh.

Uncle Bill turned toward the video camera. "Kyle, Cade, I think we've got our new target."

In the hospital room, Agent Murphy stepped forward. "Mr. Tarleton, I'll get on the horn to my people. We'll deploy hostage-rescue teams to Yellowstone Park and start combing the area."

"We'll send you coordinates of the caldera itself. Hey Branson, how big is the actual opening into the caldera?"

"It's at least thirty-five miles across. But . . . hmm, let me think about this for a minute. I think there's a steam vent there though. It's pretty small, actually. It's probably not twenty feet across."

"And does the vent lead straight down? Like a mine shaft?" Bill said.

"Well sure. Where else would it lead?"

He was met with silence.

"Sorry. Yes, it would look something like a misshapen hole twisting straight down. But it's bright yellow all around the edges. And greenish a little further down. That's caused by all the sulfur that escapes. It would be very easy to spot the steam vent from the air."

"Agent Murphy," Bill yelled, "let's get moving! We've got to locate Jarrah. We find Jarrah, we find Jana and the nuke. I'll call the president. Cade, Kyle, I can't tell you what to do. But if you can walk, Jana needs every eye she can get."

In the hospital room, Kyle looked at Cade. "You up for this, man?"

"Shut up and tell me where my damn jeans are. I hate these stupid hospital gowns."

42

AN ANCIENT BLADE

Remote cabin, Yellowstone National Park, Wyoming

Jana drifted in and out of consciousness. As she awoke, all she
could see was darkness. Then she dropped back into a swirling
blur of muted sounds, snapshots in her mind of memories from
times gone by, and a throbbing headache that felt like a migraine.
She was having trouble telling what was real and what was a
dream. And the more she tried to reason it out, the less sense
any of her thoughts made.

Voices, she thought. *Those are voices. I know I heard that.* But no
matter how hard she tried, she could not lift her eyelids. They
felt like sheets of lead pushing against her pupils. But there
were voices all right. Muted, faint, distorted, and she could
understand none of it.

Another language? she wondered. She felt tugging against her
limbs. Not rough and forceful, but it was definitely there—a
pulling sensation. As if, something, or someone, was pulling
against her arm, then her leg. It was a moment later she realized
what was happening—her clothing, someone was pulling against
her clothing, and then a blindfold was torn from her face. She
felt like she was in a drug-induced stupor, but forced her eyelids

open.

What she saw before her was grotesque. A Middle Eastern man glared at her through coal-black eyes; the smile of a madman painted his mouth. His thick, black hair, distinguishable only by a single shock of white that ran up one side, was wild and unkempt.

The man's eyes wandered across her body, and his grin widened. It was Jarrah. Jana was sure of it. It was Waseem Jarrah.

"Wipe the drool from her mouth," Jarrah said. "It disgusts me."

"Well, what can one expect from a woman," Rafael said as he laughed. "Here, here you are," he said as he wiped Jana's mouth with a towel. "Now, she's all prettied up for you, Señor Jarrah. But whatever to do with her? As for myself, I can think of something." He applied a vice grip to her jaw and she yanked against it.

Jarrah laughed. "Ah, Miss Baker. We are again face-to-face. We haven't been this close since our time together in Spain. How are you feeling? Are you glad to see me? After all, you've been looking for me for a long time. And now you've found me."

Jana's heart rate accelerated.

"Starting to wake up? From the look in your eyes, I'd say you're still feeling the effects of the fentanyl aerosol Rafael administered. But you should be coming out of it now. But then again," he said as he leaned in close to her face, "you are just a frail female. And females are meant to be put in their place," he said as he laughed, "dominated. And to think how easy it was to capture you. How readily you walked into my trap. I laid down a trail of breadcrumbs for you to follow, and they led you right where I wanted you to go. *Hounds to the hunters*, Miss Baker? Perhaps only now you see what a fool you are."

He stood back and let his eyes again roll across her form.

"A fine specimen, I must say."

It was only then that Jana looked down to find herself seated in a wooden chair and stripped down to her bra and panties. She yanked against the bindings on her wrists but could not free her hands from behind her back. Even her ankles had been lashed to the chair legs.

"Struggle, struggle," Jarrah said. "It will do you no good. Yes, I have placed you in a rather vulnerable position, haven't I, Miss Baker? You are way behind in the game, I'm afraid. And here we sit, in the middle of nowhere, hundreds of miles from where they search for you. And you are in exactly the position I like my females to be—one in which they know they are not in charge. I do not understand your country, Miss Baker. Women in places of power. It disgusts me."

Jana wrenched her hands against the bindings but knew the effort was futile. Her chest heaved under the terror of her circumstances.

Jarrah lunged forward and towered over her. His left hand crunched into her throat. "The things I should do to you."

Jana gagged against his choking grip. When he released her, she gasped to fill her lungs with air.

"Yes, the perfect female body lies before me. The perfect example of a submissive, dominated female. Yet your Christian skin repulses me. While I'd love to teach you a lesson myself, I could not tolerate the abomination of my flesh against yours."

Relief flooded over Jana as she began to realize that the sexual assault she feared was coming, would not.

Jarrah walked to a table and his hand disappeared into the pocket of a large backpack. When he pulled out the object he sought, Jana tried to scream, but the sounds came out stilted.

Jarrah flashed a grin and almost laughed. "That's what I like to see—fear. Let me show it to you up close. This is an ancient knife, once owned by the Prophet Mohammad. A sacred blade to say the least. I liberated it from its resting place in that infernal museum in Spain." He held the blade to the light. "This belongs in the service of Allah, where it started its life, not in some foreign land." He looked at Rafael. "Although not all things Spanish are to be discredited. Still, look at the thickness of the steel, Miss Baker. Look at the craftsmanship, the scrollwork on the handle. Just imagine it," he said as his eyes widened. "One of the knives owned and used by Mohammad *himself*."

Then his eyes became narrow slits.

"Perhaps you would like to see how sharp the blade is?"

Jana recoiled as he held the blade against her face.

"No? Well, there will be time for that. There will be time for a great many things, Miss Baker."

Jarrah walked behind her, circling her chair. Her neck craned as she followed his movements, almost certain he would slash her throat with the knife, then decapitate her.

He leaned close to her ear and whispered, "You searched for more information about your parents, didn't you?" His hot breath was nauseating.

Jarrah reared back in fits of laugher, then pulled a chair in front of her. As he sat, he placed the knife's razor-sharp tip against Jana's chin.

She recoiled from the pain and tried to lean her neck up. A tear rolled down her cheek. He grasped the center of Jana's bra and pulled it just enough to position the knife handle inside of it. When he released the strap, the bra held the knife upright, the blade against her chest and neck. She could not move without being cut.

"This is even more enjoyable than I imagined it. Tell me, did you search for more information about your parents?"

Jana's sobbing was low and silent. She struggled to keep her neck high enough.

"Answer me, Miss Baker, or things will not go so well for you."

"Yes," she whispered over the lump in her throat.

"And how much did you learn? Were you able to uncover the truth about them?"

She started to speak, but the blade cut a vertical slit into her throat and she winced against the pain.

"Oh, are you not able to speak freely? Such a pity. Now, perhaps you see the way a woman should be." He removed the knife and lay it on her lap. "Now, please continue."

"Did I learn the truth about my parents? Yes, but I've always known the truth about my parents. Having a father who died of cancer and a mother of a car accident is nothing to be ashamed of."

"The information gathering capabilities of the FBI, NSA, and CIA at your fingertips, and that's the best you can do?"

He grabbed a manila file folder from the table and pulled out the first sheet of paper. At the top, the paper read:

State of North Carolina, Certificate of Live Birth.
"Read the name and date of birth aloud, Miss Baker."

Jana squeezed her eyes closed to push free tears obscuring her vision. "Jana Michelle *Ames*. Born October 19, 1986. But, but . . . this isn't me."

"Oh, no? Read the names of the birth parents listed here, please."

"Father, Richard William Ames, born December 16, 1959. Mother, Lillian Baker Ames, born February 9, 1960."

"Fascinating, Miss Baker, isn't it? It is true, you do not recognize the surname *Ames*, but your father's first and middle names were Richard and William, were they not? He was born on December 16, 1959, correct? And your mother, Lillian Baker, was, in fact, born on February 9, 1960. And let's examine this date, October 19, 1986. This is *your* birth date, correct?"

Jana's mouth hung open.

Jarrah continued. "And your mother's maiden name was, in fact, Baker, was it not? Baker, the same surname of your grandfather. How very interesting. I can tell by that stupid expression on your face that you have never known the truth."

Jana shook her head and more tears streamed down her face. "No. No, this can't be. You falsified these documents! This is not my birth certificate!"

"Is it not? Yes, it would be a most disturbing revelation indeed. To discover one's entire life to be a lie."

"My life is not a lie!"

"Tell me. How is it that you were not aware of your own surname?"

"My last name is *Baker*. It's always been Baker. My parents were never married. Are you happy now? They never married. When my father died, I was two years old. That's why my last name is the same as my mother's."

"And what then, was said to be your father's name?"

"His name was Richard William."

"Richard William? Is that what your mother told you? It is true, the name of William is used in the Western world as a surname, but more commonly as a first or middle name, no? The surname of *Williams*, with an *s* on the end, is much more common. And this birth certificate says Richard William *Ames*. Hmmm, quite a coincidence that all the first names, middle names, and birth dates match up to you, your mother, and your father. Well then, let's read further, shall we? These documents are so fascinating."

He held up another. At the top, it read:

FEDERAL BUREAU OF INVESTIGATION
UNITED STATES DEPARTMENT OF JUSTICE
WASHINGTON, DC
CURRENT ARREST OR RECEIPT

Below was a mugshot and other details.

A droplet of blood rolled down Jana's throat from the cut and landed in her lap. Her eyes locked onto the mugshot.

"You look white as a sheet, Miss Baker. The face looks familiar, no? A striking resemblance to your father, isn't it? Now, read for me this part here," Jarrah said as he pointed.

Jana's voice became monotone as she read the words. "Date arrested or received, 10/29/1988. Charge or offense," Jana's body shook, "18 U.S.C. 793—US Code, Section 793: Gathering, transmitting or losing defense information." Her head leaned down into the overwhelming emotions. "No. No, this isn't my father. It isn't true!"

"But it is true, Miss Baker. The evidence is right in front of you. And having been at the top of your graduating class at Quantico, I assume this is a federal code section you are familiar with. And this *is* a federal arrest warrant, isn't it? Tell me, what does section 793 pertain to?"

"Espionage," she whispered.

"Correct, Miss Baker, espionage. Spying. And how interesting the date on this document is, October 29, 1988. You would have been two years old at the time." He put his face against hers. "That particular date is etched into your memory. Don't lie to me, Miss Baker."

"Yes," she said.

"And what does October 29, 1988 mean to you?"

"It's the date my father died." The enormity of the revelation lay upon Jana's psyche like a thousand-pound weight.

"Your honesty is refreshing. *October 29, 1988.* The date your father died. Now, perhaps, you are starting to believe. Your father didn't die on that date, Miss Baker. It's the date he was arrested, arrested for espionage against the United States."

"Nooo!" she screamed.

"Come now. You resist the truth. Your father was passing state secrets to the Russians. Made a bit of money, I believe."

Jana leaned down and sobbed.

"Your mother and father *were* married," Jarrah said as he pulled out a North Carolina certificate of marriage. "Your real name is Ames, not Baker. But I suppose your mother told you they were never married to hide the truth from you—that your father was an enemy of the state. The embarrassment of his arrest must have been overwhelming for her. Which is why I'm sure she went to all this trouble."

He held up another document. It read:

STATE OF NORTH CAROLINA

CERTIFICATE OF NAME CHANGE

"She changed your legal surname, Miss Baker. Or should I call you Miss Ames?"

"My name is Baker!"

"Your life is a lie, Miss Baker. But it's all starting to make sense to you now, isn't it? Your father had been arrested for treason and your mother wanted to disappear from it all. So she changed both of your names to her maiden name and tried to put the past behind her. It is no wonder that you weren't able to find more information about your parents. You were looking for the wrong names." His voice lowered. "I have one last document for you. But let me ask first, before today, does the surname of Ames sound at all familiar to you?"

Jana's eyes locked onto his. The name *was* familiar. The same thought had occurred to her when she found it on her own FBI personnel file, yet she could not place it.

"It's not quite coming to you? Perhaps we should try to use it in context. How about the full name of *Aldrich* Ames?"

"Aldrich? . . ."

"Aldrich Hazen Ames," he said the words as though calling role. "One of the most infamous spies of your country's history." He held another FBI arrest record in front of her. "Arrested February 21, 1994. A thirty-one-year veteran of the Central Intelligence Agency. Now, Miss Baker, take a look at the mugshot of Aldrich Ames. A striking resemblance to your father, no? A slightly older version of your father."

Jana's mouth hung agape.

"Well, let me be the first to introduce you to *Uncle Aldrich*," he said as he rocked back in maniacal laughter.

"Nooo!" Jana screamed.

"Your father is the younger brother of Aldrich Ames. After your father's arrest in 1988, the FBI took a hard look at Uncle Aldrich here. But it took eight years to build a case against him. Your father and your uncle, both enemies of the state. Makes one wonder if it runs in the family, Miss Baker."

"Lies! It's all lies!"

"Yes, and apparently, I am not the only one who had doubts about you and your lineage. The FBI knew full well who your father and uncle were when they hired you. You had not committed any crime so they had no legal basis to reject your application solely on a few bad seeds." He leaned over her, his eyes tranquil and satisfied. "You must have wondered why the bureau polygraphed you every four months instead of every six, like the rest of the agents."

"How would you know they polygraphed me every four months?"

"How I know is irrelevant to the question at hand." He began walking a slow circle around her. "And what do you think their explanation would be? Hmmm?" He stopped and grabbed her jaw. "I suppose you thought they polygraphed you so often because you worked high-profile cases? And yet no other agent received such treatment, did they?" He drew a deep breath, then belted. "They never trusted you! They never trusted your loyalty!"

"No!"

"They not only believe your loyalty is in question, they never believed you had the guts to do the job of a man."

"You filthy pig!"

He snatched the knife and straddled her and sat on her lap. They were face-to-face. His left hand yanked her hair back to expose her neck as he pressed the blade against her throat. Blood leaked onto the blade.

"Watch your tone with me, you submissive little whore. Although I may be detested at the stench emanating from your infidel skin, my friend Rafael here does not find it so repulsive."

Both men laughed in unison. Jana looked into Rafael's black eyes and saw lust.

"Yes," Rafael said as he leaned over Jana from behind the chair. "The body is firm, very firm. And it would be such a shame to slice it to pieces before sampling it."

Jarrah stood and walked to the table. He shouldered the heavy backpack, then he and Rafael walked across the creaking floor planks toward the door where Rafael unfolded a paper map.

Jarrah said, "In your scouting mission, Tower Falls is to our northwest?"

"There's no *s* on the end. You mean Tower Fall, Señor Jarrah. Yes, over in that direction," he said, pointing northwest. "But you'll simply follow Tower Creek." He placed a finger on the map. "That's the water source that feeds into this lake. It will lead you right to top of the falls, a hundred-and-thirty-two-foot drop straight down into the gorge known as Devil's Den. There are caves up there."

"Devil's Den, how appropriate." Jarrah laughed. "Distance?"

"A good two kilometers."

They exchanged a few more words, and embraced. Jarrah walked out the door and was gone.

When Rafael returned, the door closed behind him. He looked at the knife Jarrah had left on the table.

"We will wait a short time, Miss Baker," he said as he glanced at his watch. "I have my instructions. And besides, I want the effects of the fentanyl to completely wear off before we begin. I want you fully awake so you will know what is happening to you." He stood in front of her and rubbed the back side of his fingers across her cheekbone. When she recoiled, he reared his hand back and cracked it across her face. Her head jarred to the side. "But I don't want to keep you in suspense too long. My instructions are quite clear. Señor Jarrah has outlined the exact time of day and method of your death. An ancient method of flaying that was used in the time of Mohammad. It will be a first for me. But as I explained earlier, unlike you, I am very loyal to my employers and I follow their instructions to the letter." His eyes drifted across her body and he smiled. "But I have no intention of letting this body go to waste."

The last thing Jana remembered before she blacked out was

him again rearing the back of his hand.

43

PRIORITY ONE

Twin Cities Community Hospital Heliport, Templeton, California

Twelve minutes later Cade, Kyle, Agent Murphy, and the rest of hostage-rescue team six ran toward three separate Bell UH-1Y Venom Super Huey helicopters.

"How long?" Cade yelled over the thrashing rotor blades.

Agent Murphy cupped his hands around his mouth and yelled, "Jets are heating up at Oak Country Ranch Airport." He pointed Northwest. "About six clicks. We're eleven hundred miles from the caldera in Wyoming." He nodded toward a helicopter for Cade and Kyle to board.

The National Guard chopper pilot motioned for Cade and Kyle to put on headsets.

"How long is it going to take to travel eleven hundred miles?" Cade said to Kyle.

"Agent Murphy said the Gulfstream 6 we're about to board has a max speed of around seven hundred miles per hour. One hour and forty-five minutes."

"Kyle, we don't have that kind of time. We've lost so much time already. We've got to get to Jana."

"You're preaching to the choir, man. Not only that, but Jarrah will be preparing to detonate. He's driven himself out to the middle of nowhere. He's not going to sit around long."

Once the choppers touched down on the airport tarmac, all eight HRT operators sprinted toward the jet. They were packed down with weaponry of all types. Kyle and Cade boarded last. Cade leaned into the cockpit. "Pilot, let's go. Let's go right now."

"Waiting on clearance from the tower, sir. Be moving out shortly."

"Clearance from the tower, my ass!" Cade yelled. "This is NSA priority level fifteen. I *am* your clearance. Now move!"

"Yes, sir," the pilot replied as he and the copilot pushed the plane into forward motion.

When Cade strapped on a seat belt, Kyle looked at him and laughed.

"What's so funny?"

"Damn, man," Kyle said. "You're getting hard."

"You ever used one of these?" Agent Murphy said as he presented Cade with the butt end of a 9 mm Glock.

Cade's mind flashed back two years. At the time, he and Jana had fled toward the exit of the Thoughtstorm building during an FBI raid. When a guard had pointed a rifle at Jana, Cade shot the man at point-blank range. Cade reached for the Glock and a chill ran through his body. "Yes, I've used one." He yelled toward the cockpit, "Pilot, I want you at max speed as fast as physically possible. And then I want you to increase speed."

"Sir, max speed for this aircraft is .92 mach. Federal Aviation Regulations prohibit exceeding max V-speed—"

"Don't make me come up there," Cade screamed.

The pilot began to speak but thought better of it. The jet rocketed down the only runway and took flight, banking northwest. Cade felt the strong g-forces push against his body.

He held a thumbs-up to Kyle.

Thirty minutes later, a secure video uplink was established with NSA headquarters.

"Uncle Bill," Cade said into the video monitor, "what assets do we have on the ground in Yellowstone?"

"US Parks Service Rangers have fanned out across the park, looking for anything. We've also got a handful of agents from Idaho Falls, Butte, Bozeman, and Billings en route. And National Guard has a couple of Hueys moving in to meet you."

"Wait, Bill," Kyle said, "that's it?"

"Kyle, that's everything in the region. We've tasked three other hostage-rescue teams to come in from Washington, but those are the closest ones. Remember, Washington is on lockdown. All assets from around the country that are not currently deployed to an active warzone were sent to that region. You and hostage-rescue team six are the closest things we have."

"Cade," Knuckles said across the video screen, "we've retasked several satellites to scour the area of Wyoming nearest to the caldera."

"What did you find?"

"Everything and nothing. Look, this is the wilderness. It's a national park of over thirty-four hundred square miles in size. There are hikers and campers all over the place. The satellites are picking up heat signatures scattered throughout. Not many of them, mind you, because the area is so remote, but it's not like we can pinpoint exactly where to send you."

"We'll head straight for the opening of the caldera," Kyle said. "Why wouldn't we? That has to be where Jarrah is headed."

Dr. Branson leaned into view of the video monitor. "Agent MacKerron, I know what you're thinking, that Jarrah will just walk up to the mouth of the caldera and drop the weapon down the hole, but it's not that simple. The topmost magma chamber of the supervolcano is very close to the surface but the magma chamber is huge. It stretches underground for a couple of miles. If he detonates anywhere in that area, the explosion will penetrate the upper chamber which will cause a cascading effect down to the superchamber below. Once that is unleashed . . ."

"You are full of good news," Cade muttered. "Did I tell you yet that I don't like geologists?"

"No, but thanks for sharing."

Agent Murphy leaned over Kyle's shoulder. "I'm in comms with the chopper pilots that will meet us at Yellowstone Airport where we touch down. We've got two National Guard Hueys out of Driggs, Idaho, inbound at this time."

"That's impressive," Uncle Bill said.

"I'll split my team up into two units. But there's no space on those choppers for Agent MacKerron here and Mr. Williams. Sorry, boys. I've got to put my most seasoned operators into the field as first priority."

Cade stood. "What? But Jana is out there somewhere! I've got to find her."

"Sorry, son—Washington. I've got my orders. You know as well as I do that finding that device is top priority."

"Cade," Kyle said, "I don't know how to tell you, but he's right. HRT has a fairly powerful radiation detector. They'll be on the hunt for that nuclear device, not Jana."

Cade sat and buried his face in his hands. He looked at Kyle. "I can't leave her out there. I don't care what it takes. She's not going to die like that. Not like that."

"Come on. It won't be long before we're on the ground. Let's get you a Kevlar vest." Kyle turned to the HRT weapons specialist. "What can you spare?"

44

CLIPPED SILENCE

Yellowstone Airport, West Yellowstone, Montana

The tires on the Gulfstream barked onto the single runway of the remote Yellowstone Airport. FBI Hostage-Rescue Team operators burst from the cabin in a sprint toward two Bell UH-1 Huey helicopters, both with rotors thumping. Kyle and Cade stepped off the plane and stared at the choppers as they lifted off and headed in separate directions.

"Come on," Kyle said as he shouldered the sniper rifle given to him by HRT. "Let's hit that ranger station over there."

The pair jogged toward an old log cabin nestled underneath fir trees at the edge of the runway. A female park ranger stood on the porch and leaned against a wooden post. The absence of makeup added to her rugged beauty.

"Is it true?" she said.

"Every bit of it," Kyle said. "I'm Agent MacKerron, FBI. This is Cade Williams, National Security Agency. We need your help."

"I bet," she said as she tipped her hat to them. "Ranger Parker. Come on inside. Those Hueys make a hell of a racket, don't they?"

As they walked through the open wooden door, Cade spoke

first. "Ranger Parker, sounds like you've been briefed on the situation."

"I didn't really give them a choice, about whether or not they were going to brief me, I mean. Told those National Guard pilots, 'My park, my rules.'"

"Yes, ma'am. Then you know what we're up against, and what they're looking for."

"Yeah, and I know there's no point trying to evacuate the park. We'd never get the tourists out in time. It would take us a couple of days just to get the word out to them. Besides, if we don't find the bomb, there won't be a park left to evacuate. How can I help?"

"Show me where we are on that map," Kyle said as he pointed to a framed map of Yellowstone National Park on the wall. "Hostage Rescue will be sweeping an area . . . let's see, yeah, should be this grid area up here. They'll run a grid pattern all across this hill country."

"Why do they think the device is there?"

"The caldera," Cade said. "If he detonates anywhere in this grid, he'll be able to penetrate into both the upper and lower magma chambers of the supervolcano."

"Got it."

Kyle continued. "To be honest, aside from helping us get out to this locale, I don't know what else you can do for us. But maybe with your familiarity with the area, you can point us to anything that comes to mind. The psycho we're after has kidnapped one of our agents and we assume she's here. If that's true, he'd want," he looked at Cade, "somewhere private. I don't know. Is there anything in this area that jumps out at you? Any caves, cabins? Anything like that?"

"Well," Ranger Parker said, "the area you're pointing to is a somewhat remote area of the park. Not nearly the most popular area for tourists. But there's a campground right over here in the Mount Sheridan area. Lots of RVs and camp sites up and down this ridge. That's the most likely place to find people. But I overheard one of the Huey pilots talking about being assigned to sweep that area from the air, which I didn't understand, by the way. How are they going to just look out the chopper door and find the thing? Do they have some type of equipment on board they can detect a nuclear device with?

"That's right, ma'am," Cade said.

"If that area is already being covered, we should focus somewhere else. Besides," Kyle said, "if this is a campground, I'm not so sure he'd hide in there."

"Why not?"

"He'd want more privacy than that. He would need to be away from prying eyes."

"So where was the other Huey headed?" Cade asked.

"Up over here. A place called Caldera Rim."

"Aside from the obvious, what's there?"

"Just an overlook, really. See, it's on Grand Loop Road. The road runs alongside the Gibbon River. Caldera Rim is just like a small park where you can look out over the falls. Not much there, just a place to park your car and see the beauty of nature."

"Well, Kyle, it's still well within the target zone. But why did the second Huey choose this spot?"

"Sounds too obvious, you know?" Kyle replied. "A place called Caldera Rim?" He repositioned the sling of the sniper rifle higher on his shoulder and looked at the ranger. "How remote an area is the overlook at Caldera Rim?"

"Believe it or not, Grand Loop Road is a fairly busy thoroughfare. Not exactly a Los Angeles rush hour, mind you, but cars and tour buses move up and down the road all the time. To answer your question, for Yellowstone, it's not remote at all. Now if you were here in the winter, that's a different story. The road is only open during the warmer months of the year. May through November. So during winter, it's as remote as it gets."

"Kyle, that doesn't sound like the place. And there's no cabins or remote campgrounds up here? Nowhere for even an RV camper to park, out of sight? This isn't it."

"I agree," Cade said.

"Privacy, you say? Hmmm, privacy," the ranger said as she rubbed her chin. "Well, let me think. There's always the old Willmont homestead." Ranger Parker placed a finger on the map.

"What's the Willmont homestead?" Kyle said.

"1865," she replied. "If you were tourists, I'd bore you to death with the details of the old place. I used to guide hikers up there. Today, it's used as what we call a scout camp. But we haven't had to use it in years. Man named Willmont built it just after the Civil War. He settled here after Lincoln was shot. Thought the country was going to hell."

"He was right," Cade said. "It's an old house?"

"Cabin. About the same size as the one you're standing in. But this one is much newer."

"Newer?" Kyle said as he glanced at the layer of thick dust coating the exposed ceiling joists. "This thing looks like it might fall down any minute."

"Watch it," Ranger Parker said, though she was grinning. "I was a little girl when my father helped build this cabin. He was a ranger, too."

"Don't pay him any mind," Cade offered. "No one likes him very much."

She glanced Kyle up and down. "I doubt that."

"You said the scout camp hasn't been used in years?"

"Yeah, we try to maintain the scout camps that we have, but there are only a couple of them. They're really only there in case we have a winter rescue and we need shelter."

Cade leaned in and squinted at the map. "That's in the middle of nowhere. No easy road access, no tourists, and a cabin, hidden away from prying eyes."

"It would take us forever to drive over in that direction, then make the hike out there, Cade."

But Cade was preoccupied in a thought. "What's this little body of water on the map, just east of the cabin?"

"Wrangler Lake. Compared to the park's main lake, it's a speck on the map."

He walked to the open door and looked out at the only other building on the edge of the airstrip. The tail section of a small plane hung just within view.

"How big is Wrangler Lake?"

"Tiny," she said. "I don't know. Maybe a thousand feet from one side to the other? Maybe two."

"Is that a float plane in the hangar?"

"A De Havilland Canada DHC-3. Why?"

He turned to face Ranger Parker. "We're going to need to commandeer it, ma'am. And we need you to give us a ride."

"What makes you think I'm a pilot?"

"Only a pilot would be able to identify the exact type of aircraft that is."

She smiled then said, "Was afraid you were going to say that. Let's go." The group headed out the door.

Once airborne, Kyle keyed his headset and said, "It's a good thing you can fly. Is there much need for a float plane here in the park?"

Under a sudden downdraft, the plane dipped and Cade made a sound from the rear seat as his stomach dropped.

"Oh, ah, no. We don't fly very much. We do it occasionally, of course. But the plane is more or less reserved for emergencies."

"Like this?"

"Well, this is certainly an emergency. But, no, our emergencies don't typically involve lunatics with nuclear weapons. Ours are more the type where a hiker has broken a leg and has to be extracted off a hillside or something."

"That doesn't sound good," Kyle said. "Happen often?"

"Oh, those are the easy ones."

"What are the hard ones?"

Parker looked at Kyle and shook her head. "Grizzlies. There's the occasional mauling."

"Grizzlies. Wonderful. I think I like my job better than yours."

"So if you don't fly that often, how much flight time do you have?" Cade said.

She began counting with her fingers. "This will be my fiftieth."

"Fiftieth? Fifty hours of flight time? Doesn't it take forty to get your single-engine solo license?"

"Yep," she said as a gust of wind torqued the tail section to the left.

"But," Cade continued, "if you only have fifty hours of flight time, that means you don't have your commercial license. You aren't allowed to fly anyone."

"That's right," she said as she laughed. "Still think flying out to Wrangler Lake and attempting a water landing is such a good idea?"

Cade leaned from the cramped space behind her and said, "Wait, you *have* done a water landing, right?"

"Nope. First time."

"Kyle?" Cade said. "Remind me to kill Uncle Bill when we get back. I'm not cut out for this crap."

"Just focus on Jana, man. Hey, Parker, what's our best approach to the cabin? Once we're on foot, which side can we approach from high ground?"

"You might want to approach it from the north."

The plane cut to the right and followed a mountain road below until a small body of water was in sight. Kyle turned and tucked the sniper rifle in between the two seats in an effort to cushion it from any jarring as they landed on the surface of the water.

"What was all that about the high ground?" Cade said.

"Cade, you know as well as I do that this is a wild goose chase, right? Anyway, the high ground is something used to our tactical advantage. We'd rather approach a structure from a higher vantage point."

"Gone all tactical on us, haven't you?"

"Yeah, man. Can't say as I relish the idea of spending my career working the business end of a raid. You know, knocking down doors every day. But it's a kick of adrenaline, that's for sure."

The plane descended but bounced back up. "Sorry. Sorry about that. You can't see it from here, but the cabin is just over that ridge. Just west of the lake."

"We're going to need you to stay with the plane," Kyle said.

"What? You guys need me. You two don't look like you spend much time in the woods, if you know what I mean."

"You have any equipment on board? Radios, anything? If we run into trouble, we'll need you to call the cavalry."

She turned toward Cade. "Reach behind you, in the survival pack. There's a handheld radio. Should be all charged up. Agent MacKerron, open up that topo map and let's have a look."

Kyle studied the map of the surrounding hillsides and forest.

"Okay, here we go," she said as she pointed to the map. "I'm going to try to land on the water on this side, and taxi toward the western edge. That will put you on the closest side of the lake to the cabin."

"You just concentrate on setting this thing down in one piece," Kyle said.

Ranger Parker performed a gentle turn to the left and descended to just above treetop level. To Kyle, it looked as though they might brush the tops of the conifers. Then from the engine came a loud pop, followed by a sputtering sound.

"Oh shit," Parker said as she vice-gripped the controls. "Hang on, everybody." The plane dipped, regained power, then the engine sputtered once more and dropped into clipped silence. "Hang on!" she yelled.

45

BLANKET OF ANONYMITY

Remote cabin, Yellowstone National Park, Wyoming

Jana's eyes opened and she squinted into bright afternoon sun piercing the cabin's window. The right side of her neck was tight with pain from her head's being in that position for so long, and her jaw throbbed. When she saw Rafael, she wrenched her body upright.

"Enjoy your little nap? Let me look at your pupils." He leaned toward her. "Very nice. I'd say most of the effects of the fentanyl have worn off. Good, this is how I want you. I want you fully conscious and aware as I run my hands across you." His grin sent a nauseating sensation through Jana. "And other things." He began to pace the floor in front of her. "But first, there are some things I want to know from you. Things about your terrorism investigation that make me curious. For example, during your failed investigation last year that concluded with Jarrah detonating a device outside of your CIA headquarters, were you aware of my involvement in the plot?"

"I'm not telling you anything."

"Oh, come now, Miss Baker. Everyone in your FBI expects you to betray your country already. What can it hurt?"

"Fuck you!"

"You will tell me a great many things. After all, you will be dead soon and I will be on my way out of the country." He pulled a chair close to her and sat. "I want to know if the FBI knew about me last year. You see, I make quite an effort to remain off the grid. It helps me to maintain my anonymity, if you know what I mean."

"Go screw yourself," she lashed.

"That's quite a foul mouth for someone in your position. I bet you won't be saying things like that in a few minutes when I am having my fun with you." He grabbed her jaw and squeezed. "Tell me! Does the FBI know about me?"

Jana yanked and thrashed but could not free herself. When he finally let go, the enormity of the danger she was in sent a shock of adrenaline through her body. Jana shook her head and her breathing accelerated.

Rafael looked at her chest as it moved up and down and he smiled. "So very nice, Miss Baker. I do believe I will enjoy your body very much. Very much indeed. Again, what harm can come if you tell me what you know? Was the FBI aware that I transported the suicide bomber last year, along with his weapon, from one place to another?"

When she did not respond, he raised an open hand and slapped her face with force.

Jana coughed. "We knew there was someone, someone involved in transport. But," she coughed again, "we did not know who it was."

"And what about now? What does the FBI know about my involvement in the assassinations leading up to today?"

Jana glared at the man then said through gritted teeth, "Your involvement? You have something you'd like to tell me?"

He reared back in laughter. "True to the end, Miss Baker. True to the end. Still think you're an FBI agent working a terrorism case, don't you? Still think you can save the day? How wonderful. And I seem to have touched a chord as well. Perhaps you did not know I assassinated that pathetic sheriff in Louisiana, the director of the CDC, and the director of the FBI."

Jana yanked against her restraints and screamed, "I'm going to kill you!"

He reared a hand and slapped her back down.

"Yes, I have touched a chord indeed. It's the director of the FBI, isn't it? Closer to him than I realized, weren't you? I must say that it is quite enthralling to see you squirm. You will make quite a play toy. And afterward, to slice the flesh from your body. Such a shame. It will be quite the waste. But since your time is close, I will share with you the more intimate details about your precious FBI director's death. I practiced quite a bit with the crossbow. I had never fired one, you see. But I have to admit, seeing the crossbow bolt sail across the street and rip its way into the brain of my prey was an adrenaline rush. Surely you saw the crime-scene photos. There was a most beautiful spray of brain matter on the sidewalk."

"Shut up! Shut up! Shut your mouth!"

He jammed a hand onto her throat and squeezed.

46

MOTION

Wrangler Lake, Yellowstone National Park, Wyoming. About thirty-three miles west of Yellowstone Airport.

The single-engine plane dropped, clipped the tip of a pine tree, and pitched into a slight sideways yaw just as it cleared the tree line.

"Hang on!" Ranger Parker yelled as she jammed her foot onto the left rudder pedal to correct the spin. The plane lurched onto the water's surface with a heavy thud. They all slammed forward into their seat belts as the plane skidded across the water and began to slow. When it came to a stop, a wall of water washed over the plane's windshield and everything was again quiet.

"Shit," the ranger said as she panted.

"You okay, Cade?" Kyle said.

"Yeah. You?"

"Thanks Parker, you saved our asses. Come on, Cade, we've got to get out of this flying coffin. We're on the wrong side of the lake from the cabin, right?"

"Yes, ouch. Shit, that hurts" Parker said through gritted teeth. "It's right over that ridge. In the unlikely event anyone is in the cabin, I doubt we are close enough for them to have heard the plane approaching."

"What is it? You hurt?" Kyle said.

"There's no time," Parker replied. "I'll be fine. I didn't need that leg anyway. You need to get to the cabin."

Kyle leaned over her. "Parker, that leg is broken. We need to get you out of here."

"What for? The plane floats. It's not like it's going anywhere."

"Let's try the radio," Cade said. "Can you raise your base station?"

"No engine, no radio. Sorry." Parker said. "And that handheld would have to be taken up to the top of one of these ridges to do any good."

"We're cut off," Kyle said. "Wonderful. There's no way to call the outside world."

"Well," Parker said, "no use crying over spilled engine parts and broken legs. I still have jurisdiction in this park. You two get the hell off my plane."

Kyle shook his head. "Come on, Cade. Time to get wet."

"Don't let the radio submerge," Parker yelled. "You can use the flotation device to rest your rifle on as you swim to shore."

A few minutes later, Cade and Kyle trudged out of the lake and looked back at the plane where Ranger Parker flashed them a thumbs-up. They then began to jog along the shoreline. The run continued up the small ridge until they neared the top.

"That was one tough woman," Kyle said as he unshouldered his rifle and held up his hand in a closed fist.

"What the hell is that closed fist supposed to mean?" Cade whispered.

"It means to stop, nimrod. Down there. Look, there's the cabin. Ranger Parker knows her terrain," he said as he lay on his stomach. "She's put us on the high ground for our approach."

Kyle peered through the scope of the sniper rifle, then twisted the reticle to zoom the view closer.

"What are we waiting for?" Cade said. "Let's go. What if she's in there?"

"Sit tight. We have to know what we're walking into. What if she is in there, but we kick down the door and get cut in half with a shotgun? Wouldn't be able to help her much then. Besides, Cade, Jarrah is the priority."

"Maybe to you. What do you see through the optics?"

"Nothing. I can see through that side window, but I don't see any movement. And judging from the way the porch looks, there hasn't been anyone in there in a long time."

"You mean she's not there?"

"Doesn't look like anyone is there, no. I can't see anything on the ground leading up to the porch steps that looks disturbed. You know, there are leaves all over the steps. No one has cleared them off. There are no fallen branches pushed to the side, no—"

"No what?"

"I just saw something. Motion. In the window. I was looking at the porch steps, but . . . it could have just been a reflection of a bird flying over or something. But I thought I saw motion out of the corner of my eye. Probably imagining things. I don't know. Come on, let's slide over to our right. I might get a better view."

47

FEAR

Remote cabin, Yellowstone National Park

This time when Rafael slapped Jana's face, she tasted salty wetness in her mouth.

"Coward," she said. Then she spat blood onto the floor. "A coward ties up his victim, then acts as if he's all-powerful."

"Jarrah would have sliced you limb from limb by now. As it is, I have other interests." He stood behind her chair and leaned over her, burying his face into her neck.

"Get off of me, you filthy prick!"

"Oh, but Miss Baker. Let's get to know one another better. We are going to be very close."

He walked around in front of her and picked up the antique knife and placed the blade against her cheek.

"You will learn to be more respectful."

He wove the blade underneath her chin, then down to the top of her shoulder where it stopped, its tip just underneath Jana's bra strap. He flicked the blade to the side and the razor-sharp edge sliced the strap.

48

RIGHTS DELIVERED

On a hillside above a remote cabin, Yellowstone National Park

"Come on, man! What can you see now?"

Kyle shifted his body and again peered through the scope. As he zoomed his view through the window, his shoulders tensed. "Oh shit! She's there! There's a man with a knife. He's cutting at her clothing!"

Cade started to jump up but Kyle wrenched him down.

"Get off of me!"

"Cade, we have to take him by surprise. I barely have a view of him. And there might be others in that cabin with her."

"But they're going to hurt her!"

"Listen, and do exactly as I say. As quickly and as quietly as you can, get down there and get onto the porch by the door. You can't be detected. Once you're there, wait for the shot. If I get an opening, I'll take the son of a bitch out, then I'll come charging down the hill. You get in there as soon as you hear me fire." He pulled Cade's face close to his. "You up for this?"

Cade pulled out the Glock. "You just do your part. I'm going to rip out his liver and eat it with some fava beans and a nice Chianti."

"Good. Time to meet the dragon."

Cade slid down the hill and crept onto the porch, then leaned against the plank siding.

Kyle drew in several deep breaths, then exhaled in a long, slow action. His cheek never lifted from the rifle stock.

He glanced at Cade, who nodded back.

Cade heard a chilling scream come from inside the cabin and his adrenaline raged. He whispered, "Come on, Kyle. Shoot, dammit. Shoot." He looked up at Kyle and moved in front of the wooden door. "Shot or no shot, I'm going in."

Up on the hilltop, Kyle could see bits of motion through the glass, but he had no clear line of sight. He couldn't even tell what he would be shooting at. But as he heard the scream, he knew. He had to risk it. Then a flash of motion popped into view and he touched off a round. The rifle recoiled against his shoulder and he leapt to his feet and tore down the hill.

Cade kicked the door so hard it burst open and dislodged from one of its hinges. He saw Jana tied to a chair and a dark-haired male covered in his own blood, standing back up. The man raised a handgun and fired at Cade, and Cade fired back. Both men spun sideways as the force of the bullets hit home. Rafael rocked backward, fell against the table, and collapsed to the ground. He then glared at the two bullet holes, one in his upper chest, the other in his hip.

Kyle burst through the open door just as Rafael raised his gun again and fired. Kyle took the full force of the bullet in his abdomen, then flash-fired his rifle at point blank range. The bullet struck Rafael's forearm, causing the handgun to spin across the floor. Kyle stood, then looked around the room to ensure no other terrorists were present. He towered over Rafael and clutched a hand against his own ribs.

Jana screamed. "Cade! Kyle! You're hit. You're both hit!"

Cade looked at his right shoulder to find blood streaming down. The pistol dropped to the ground from a hand which no longer seemed to have the ability to grip the handle. He went to Jana and began pulling against the bindings on her wrists. "Are you okay?" he said.

Her face was flush and blood dripped from the side of her mouth and neck.

"Yes." She looked down at the torn bra that barely covered her. "The son of a bitch."

Rafael watched from the floor as he applied pressure to his chest. Frothy, red blood spurted from one of the bullet holes. It was a lung shot.

"He won't be hurting you any more, Jana," Kyle said as he stood over the man.

"Cade, are you all right? Can you untie my hands? He was going to," she started to cry. "He was going to . . ."

Rafael laughed at her until he coughed.

"I know," Cade said as he fought her bindings free, then applied pressure to the wound on his shoulder. "It's all over now. Like Kyle said. He's not going to touch you now."

"So amusing, your country," Rafael said.

Kyle placed the muzzle of the rifle onto Rafael's temple and pushed. "Amusing? How amusing do you think it is now?"

He peered at Kyle through the sides of his eyes. "You will not hurt me. You are a police officer."

"Federal agent, dickwad," Kyle said.

"You are bound by your laws to get me medical care. I'll be in a hospital. You will save me so I can stand trial. What a wonderful country you have. But make no mistake, you will not stop him." He laughed and blood dripped down the side of his mouth. "You will not stop Jarrah. It is too late."

Jana stood and rubbed her wrists.

"Why don't you shut the fuck up?" she said.

Cade slumped to the ground and his eyes rolled to the back of his head.

"Cade!" Kyle yelled. He dropped down to Cade and began to apply pressure to his wound.

But Jana grabbed Cade's Glock off the floor and discharged three rounds into Rafael's chest.

Kyle recoiled. "Jana!" he yelled and began to reach out to her.

But it was too late. Rafael was dead. She looked at Kyle with eyes of cold steel and said through gritted teeth, "Fuck him." She stood atop the carcass. "After all, he has the right to remain silent." She fired another round into his chest. "He has the right to an attorney." She pumped a round into his groin. "If he cannot afford an attorney, one will be appointed for him." She squeezed the trigger in repetition until she had emptied the magazine into his chest and groin area. Brass shell casings littered the floor and the smell of gunpowder and blood hung thick in the air.

She yelled at the dead man, "DO YOU UNDERSTAND THESE RIGHTS?"

Jana let the gun dangle from her fingers but otherwise stood tall.

Kyle's mouth hung agape. "Jana . . . that was an unarmed suspect. You killed an unarmed man."

"Got what he deserved!"

Kyle bent over into the pain of his own wound but otherwise kept pressure on Cade's.

"Cade's hit badly," he said

"Me?" Cade whispered through closed eyes. "I'll be fine."

"Keep pressure on his shoulder, Kyle. What about you? Let me see that." She lifted Kyle's Kevlar vest and uncovered an entrance wound just below the vest in his lower abdomen. "Here, put pressure here."

"Hey, pull that chair over here, will you? We need to elevate his legs."

Jana moved the chair while holding one hand over her exposed chest. She then wiped the blood from her face. "I'm going after him."

"Jana," Cade coughed. "You can't shoot an unarmed—"

"I said he got what he deserved! I don't want to hear another word about it. You got me?"

Jana walked toward a pile of her own clothing, then glanced back at their wounds. "I said keep pressure on this. Right here." She pointed to Kyle. "And with him, blood is spurting out with each of his heartbeats. The bullet clipped an artery. Don't move your thumb from that bullet hole. If you keep pressure on it, he won't bleed out."

"Jana," Cade said as he reached for her. "Don't leave me."

Kyle looked at her. "He doesn't stand a chance unless you get help. Get to the lake, the ranger has a medical kit in the plane."

"What time is it?" Jana said as she quickly finished dressing.

"What time is it?" Kyle replied as he looked at his watch. "It's zero nine sixteen hours. Why?"

She yanked against the broken wooden door and wrenched it out of the way. "No time for that. He detonates in two hours."

"Cade needs help, and you don't even know where Jarrah is going," Kyle said. But Jana was already out the door and down the porch steps.

She didn't turn back, but said, "Yes I do. I know exactly where he's going. I overheard their conversation."

"You can't face him alone!" Kyle yelled to her.

"I *have* to face him alone," was her solemn reply.

49

SCARS THAT SPEAK

Just north of the Willmont Homestead

Jana charged up the hillside and slung the sniper rifle diagonally over her head and shoulder as her legs pounded up the rocky terrain.

Her mind flashed back to all those times at Quantico when her instructors yelled for her to charge up a daunting hill that FBI trainees had nicknamed the widow-maker. Then another memory ricocheted forward—her shooting instructor's steely voice. *Double tap, center mass, then one to the head.*

She crested the hilltop and looked into the shimmering reflection of lake water below. On the far side of the lake, Jana saw the float plane. Her eyes continued to trace the shoreline until she found the mouth of Tower Creek. Before she broke into a sprint toward the creek, she couldn't help but notice Ranger Parker, soaked from head to foot, seated on the ground with one leg stretched in front of her. She held a rope that was attached to the plane, and dug her one good foot into the thick mud in order to pull the floating aircraft closer to shore.

My kind of woman, Jana thought.

As Jana turned to sprint toward the wide creek to follow Jarrah, she said, "This one is for me," though no one could have heard her.

Once over the hilltop, she slowed to a jog, pacing herself for the rugged run ahead. She trudged across the tilted terrain, bracing every few steps as her footing gave way underneath loose rock. To Jana, Tower Creek looked more like a river. Not the kind frequented by whitewater rafters, but a rocky fast-mover nonetheless.

She ran through thick briers, slipped on the rocky, tree-covered hillside with frequency, and collected an increasing series of scrapes and bruises as she powered forward. Although her lungs burned and her legs bled, Jana accepted the pain without a second thought.

The mission became more and more clear in her mind. Jarrah had no intention of passing the duty of detonating the nuclear device to another jihadist. He *was* the jihadist. He would do this himself, and die in the process.

Blood streamed down her shin from a fresh gash earned against the sharp rocks. Sweat rolled down her face, and the drops cleared streaks through the dirt and dried blood. The more exhausted she became, the harder she ran. But the stress and terror of what she'd just been through took its toll, and her mind wandered back to the first time she'd faced one of Waseem Jarrah's nuclear devices. In that instance, she'd broken into a similar sprint moments before detonation and engaged the suicide bomber with gunfire at point blank range. Jana now knew the horror of those events would never leave her. The bullet scars she had earned that day would make sure of that, terrifying calling cards from the bright blue morning that nearly ended in her death. The scars would always remain in her sight, every time she looked in the mirror. The scars spoke to her, like echoes from a shimmering nightmare. They would not be silenced for the rest of her life.

The sounds from that day's echoing gunfire reverberated in her head. As her feet pounded the hillside, Jana's mind descended deeper and deeper, back to the scene. In her mind's eye she could see the muzzle of the terrorist's handgun as the barrel flashed, then flashed again as he fired at her. She relived the feeling of the bullets as they slammed into her chest, smelled the acrid gunpowder, and relived the shock of blue sky she saw as her head slammed into the hard ground.

Here in an all-out sprint to stop Jarrah, Jana's vision began to blur and although she did not know it, her breathing accelerated. She was falling into a post-traumatic stress episode, and she had no control over it. Roaring sounds from the nearby river began to escalate in volume—she was nearing the waterfall.

Her feet pounded faster, the periphery of her eyesight faded further, and darkness descended upon her. It was then that she ran straight into a solid object, taking the strike at throat level—the effect something like running in a full sprint into a taught clothesline.

Her head and neck wrenched backward and her legs flew out from under her. She crashed onto her spine, and her head slammed into a rock. The wind left her lungs and her spine screamed in agony against the rifle strapped in place there.

The shockwave of pain snapped her away from the washy etchings of her PTSD episode and back to reality. Her mouth hung open but no sounds emerged. She gulped in an effort to bring oxygen back into her lungs. And standing above her was a man, a man named Waseem Jarrah.

50

THE DEVIL'S DEN

The top of Tower Fall, just above Devil's Den, Yellowstone National Park

Jarrah laughed so hard that he braced his hands onto his knees. "Ah, Miss Baker. How pleasant it is to see you again."

Jana coughed, then spit out more blood. Her chest heaved under the exhaustion of pushing her body to the breaking point.

"I wish I had been able to video that. Not that anyone would have ever seen it. Not after I complete my final objective, that is. It looked rather painful, Miss Baker. Was it?" He laughed again.

Jana wheezed and started to realize the enormity of the situation. She tried to sit up but knew she had cracked at least one rib and possibly a vertebra.

"Why don't you go fuck yourself," she choked out.

"You apparently did not learn respect from my friend Rafael. I made it clear to you, the female will bow to the male, as you do now. How you escaped Rafael's grip, I do not know. But I no longer care."

"Rafael squealed like a little girl when I killed him."

He reached underneath her and pulled against the rifle barrel, wrenching it free as Jana screamed in pain. She coughed blood, which splattered out around her mouth and chin.

He checked the rifle's chamber to ensure a round was in it, then placed his boot on her ribs and leaned his weight into her. She struggled to breathe and reached to her holster, but Jarrah slapped her hand away, then removed the Glock.

"You will have no need for this now." He flung the handgun over the edge of the gorge and watched it disappear into the mist pouring up from the bottom of the falls. He then rested the butt of the rifle on his hip.

"Devil's Den, they call it. Over a hundred feet straight down, Miss Baker. Makes a wonderful place to drop a nuclear bomb, don't you think? The explosion will originate much closer to the supervolcano that sleeps just below us." His grin widened.

Jana reached behind herself to rub the agony screaming in her back, and she groaned under the pain.

"Perhaps you would like to join it when I drop the backpack over the edge? Maybe when you were a little girl growing up on your grandfather's farm, you wondered what it would be like to be a bird? And perhaps even now, you would like to learn how to fly? Come, Miss Baker. Let's see if you can fly."

As he leaned down and grabbed the neckline of her shirt, Jana plunged a knife deep into his chest. Jarrah recoiled and fell to his back, then Jana rolled onto her hands and crawled toward him.

Jarrah's mouth and eyes opened wide and Jana straddled her legs over his abdomen and pinned his arms underneath her weight. Blood dripped from her mouth onto his sweat soaked shirt. She locked both hands around the handle of the ancient knife, it's blade still buried in his chest, and watched as fear and shock built in his coal-black eyes.

"Remember this?" Jana said through clenched teeth. "The knife that belonged to the Prophet Mohammad?"

Jarrah's eyes locked onto the knife handle and his chest heaved.

"You wanted it put to good use, as I recall. You wanted Rafael to use it to skin me alive, is that right? Like I said, Rafael squealed like a little girl when I killed him, just like the other terrorist pricks of yours I killed."

Jarrah gritted his teeth as anger and terror boiled within him.

"But you won't get the chance to squeal like they did," Jana said. She yanked the knife out of Jarrah's chest and blood spurted from the wound with each beat of his heart. She raised the blade to her side and slashed it across his throat. The razor-sharp edge sliced the soft flesh and trachea, spraying blood across the pine needles that covered the ground. Jarrah's throat lay open as he thrashed underneath her.

"You'll not be meeting Allah this day," Jana stammered. "You'll be visiting the Devil's Den!" She plunged the knife into Jarrah's chest again. "Want to learn how to fly?" she said as she belly-rolled Jarrah over the edge of the cliff and watched his body plunge one hundred thirty-two feet onto the rocks below.

51

HALO

Top of Tower Fall

A helicopter gunship swung into the mouth of the Devil's Den gorge, and an FBI sniper leaned out the open door. Jana was seated upright against the base of a pine tree and watched the chopper hover at eye-level to her. The thumping rotor sounds reverberating out of the canyon were so loud they drowned out the roar of the waterfall. The sniper was focused on something at the bottom of the falls and his hand closed into a fist, signaling the pilot to stop and hover.

He raised the rifle and aimed through the scope, but upon seeing the lifeless, blood-soaked body of Waseem Jarrah, torn and contorted across the rocks, he saw no need to fire. The man was dead. He and the other three operators in the gunship raised binoculars to scan the rim of the canyon.

When one made eye contact with Jana, she raised her forearm. It was the most she could do without causing a cascading shockwave of pain to shoot from either the broken ribs or vertebra. The chopper pilot increased his elevation and moved into a position just above the treetops over Jana's head.

First one operator, then a second, rappelled from the open

chopper through the canopy of pine boughs and branches.

The man shouldered his automatic weapon and knelt beside her. "Agent Baker? Is that our suspect at the bottom of the gorge?"

She nodded her ascent.

"Is the device in that rucksack?"

She nodded again. The second HRT operator ripped open the large backpack and began to inspect the contents.

"How badly are you hurt?"

Jana looked at his face, but sunlight pierced through the trees from behind and silhouetted him into a glow. She put a hand on his cheek.

"I can feel your face," she said.

"Yes, ma'am?"

"Sorry. Had to check if you were real or an angel."

A backboard was lowered from the hovering craft.

"Oh, I can assure you I'm real. And certainly not an angel." He almost laughed. "Going to get this neck brace on you, all right? Then you're going to take a ride on this stretcher. Let's get you laid flat. But first, how about we get a little morphine on board? Should take the edge off."

She felt a sharp sting in her thigh as he squeezed the bolus of morphine into her leg.

The second agent flashed a thumbs-up to him—the nuclear device was not armed, and the agent spoke into his comm set.

Jana's pain began to abate as a warm haze fell upon her. The men slid her into place on the hard board, then strapped her down.

She looked at the first agent's cobalt blue eyes. "You sure you're not an angel?"

"More than positive, ma'am. My mother can assure you of that fact."

"We don't have time . . . I left them . . ." She tried to sit up.

"Ma'am? Don't have time for what? Everything is okay now. The nuclear weapon is safe. There's nothing to worry about."

"Leave me here. You have to get to Agent MacKerron and Cade Williams. They're in critical—"

"Already taken care of, ma'am. The other Huey has a medic on board. They're en route to triage. They're going to be fine."

"But how did they—"

"Shhh. Try not to talk now. They said the park ranger drug herself to the top of the hillside so she could radio for help. All with a broken leg."

The warmth of morphine washed over her and she smiled. "There was a medic on board the other gunship?"

"Yes, ma'am. All HRT teams have a medic."

"And you? Are you a medic?"

"No, ma'am. We split the team into two groups, half in each chopper. They got the medic."

"So you don't really know what you're doing, do you?" Jana smiled. "If I asked you how I was doing, you'd probably tell me I'm going to be just fine, wouldn't you?"

"Yes, ma'am, I would, because you are."

"Maybe it's the morphine talking, but I'd have to agree with you. I'd say everything is going to be just fine."

52

TO LEARN THE TRUTH

Big Sky Medical Center, Big Sky, Montana. About fifty-nine miles northwest of Tower Fall

Jana woke in the hospital and opened her eyes to see a man with a grizzled beard standing beside her bed.

"More orange snack crackers, Uncle Bill?" she said as she reached to pluck a crumb free.

"They're my favorite."

"I thought Misses Uncle Bill wouldn't let you have them anymore. Presumably because of all the crumbs everywhere."

"She doesn't. But when I came out here on temporary duty to see my girl, I figured, what the hell."

Jana's eyes widened. "Kyle? Cade—"

Bill held up his hands. "They're okay. They're going to be just fine. In fact, we're all going to be just fine. We almost lost Cade. But both Cade and Kyle came out of surgery and are doing well. They're already up and walking around. Well, hobbling around, anyway."

"Jarrah?" Jana said, still trying to piece together the events.

"Dead. Very dead."

Jana thought back to the scene at the top of the waterfall and the hellish fight with Jarrah.

"How long have I been out?"

"Two days. And you'll need to stay a few more until you're able to travel. It'll be a medical transport back to Bethesda, I'm afraid."

"Bethesda Medical Center. Crap. I really don't like that place."

"I know. But it will take a bit of rehab to get you back up and running."

"I left them, Bill. I left Cade and Kyle to die."

"You made a choice."

"I should have gotten the medical kit to them."

"And if you had, what do you think would have happened?"

Jana's eyes drifted out the open doorway. "It would have been too late. Too late to stop Jarrah."

"You did what you had to do. You chose the mission over all else."

"So today is May third? And I've been unconscious for two days? We were almost too late, Bill. Did you notice the date?"

Bill exhaled. "Yes, I noticed the date. Two days ago was May first."

"May first. He was going to detonate at 11:16 a.m."

Bill nodded. "Adjusted for local time, May first, 11:16 a.m. Pacific would have been the exact date and time of the anniversary of the Osama bin Laden assassination. From what the HRT operators said, you probably killed Jarrah within minutes of then."

"I don't think I can do this anymore, Bill."

Bill studied her face a moment. "Jana, you're like a daughter to me. The daughter I never had. You need to do what's best for you."

"Bill? I don't know why I never asked you this. Did you and

Mrs. Tarleton ever have children?"

"Sure we did. A boy. He turned sixteen today."

"Oh, Bill. You shouldn't be here with me. You should be at home with him, celebrating. Sixteen is a big deal."

"At home? What for? He's right here," Bill said as he looked into the hallway.

Knuckles walked in.

"Wait a minute. Knuckles? He's your son?"

"Well, sure he is. You didn't know that? I call him *son* all the time."

"Bill, you call every male who's younger than you *son*."

Knuckles said, "Yeah, I guess we do keep it a bit of a secret. Not that I mind keeping it a secret. You think I want people to know this is my old man?"

Jana giggled, but grabbed her ribs. "Ouch. Hey, don't make me laugh, all right?"

"Listen, Jana, I just wanted to be here to see that you were all right." The boy looked at Uncle Bill. "I'll let you two talk now."

After Knuckles shut the door behind him, Bill said, "He's a good kid, really. But don't tell him I said that."

"It'll be our secret, Bill." She drew in a shallow breath and winced against the pain. "Bill, there are some things I have to know."

He looked at her, but said nothing.

"Things about my personnel file."

"You accessed it, didn't you?"

"Yes. Bill, Jarrah told me everything, had the documents to prove it. I have to know, Bill. I have to know if it's true."

He did not hesitate. "It's true."

"Which parts?"

"All of them. It's all there in your personnel file. I have access

251

to the redacted sections in the records."

"You mean when I was hired, the FBI knew my real father was Richard Ames? The brother of Aldrich Ames? And they still hired me? They let me be a special agent with a background like that?"

"Yes, the bureau knew. But Jana, you were a toddler when your father was arrested. The bureau may be a, well, a bureaucracy, but they have common sense, too."

"Yet they chose to polygraph me more frequently than anyone else. They never really trusted me, did they?"

He said nothing.

"I don't even know who I am anymore."

"I know exactly who you are. You are Jana Baker."

"But who is that? She's a work of fiction. An imagined person."

"That's crap and you know it. Jana, we are not made up of the sum total of our biological parts. *We make ourselves.* Your father had no say in the matter. He didn't form you then, and he doesn't form you now. The bureau's trust or lack of trust has no say in the matter either. *You* formed you. You are exactly who you were when you started as a rookie agent. You just have to accept your past now."

He took her hand and encased it in both of his. "There's more," he said.

"I don't think I want to hear this."

"You have to know the truth, Jana." He gripped her hand harder. "It's about your mother."

"Please don't tell me she committed treason, too," she said as a lump formed in her throat.

"Far from it." He paused. "Your mother acted as a material witness in federal court against your father. She's the reason he was convicted. She took a huge risk, Jana. She took a huge risk .

. ."

"Bill, what are you not telling me?"

His eyes found the floor. "And they killed her for it."

"Killed . . . she wasn't killed in a car accident?"

"It was a setup, Jana. It was staged to be a car accident. She was murdered."

"Who? Who killed my mother?"

"His sponsors. Your father, Richard Ames, was career CIA. But he was selling information to the Russians. After his conviction, the Russians wanted to send a message to anyone that might want to help convict another one of their spies. They killed her."

He held her hand until the sobbing subsided.

She wiped a tear from her cheek. "You talk about my father as if he's still alive."

"He *is* alive, Jana."

"What?"

"He's in the same place he's been since his conviction, at the United States Penitentiary at Florence, Colorado."

"He's alive?"

"That's right. It's called the Alcatraz of the Rockies. It houses those in the federal prison system who are deemed the most dangerous or in need of the tightest control."

Jana sat with the information for what seemed like an eternity. Her gaze fixed on the wall in front of her, though she didn't really focus on it.

"What do I do now, Bill?" she whispered. "Where do I go?"

Bill's smile almost protruded from underneath the enormity of his beard. "On." He leaned over and kissed her forehead. "You go on."

53

AFTERMATH

In the weeks and months that followed, Jana was questioned on multiple occasions by the assistant US attorney about the circumstances surrounding the death of one Gerardo "Rafael" Soto. She told the truth, all of it.

Special Agent Kyle MacKerron returned to duty leading a new team of CIA agents working counterterrorism cases. Cade Williams, as well, returned to work as an analyst at NSA on Uncle Bill Tarleton's team.

Special Agent Jana Baker spent six weeks in rehabilitation at the Bethesda Medical Center in Maryland, a hospital she was all too familiar with. She spent much of that time deep in thought, reliving the terrifying events over and over in her mind. Worst were the nights. Alone in the hospital room, Jana often awoke in the throws of a recurring nightmare, a nightmare she could not shake. It was her mind's twisted version of the experiences two years prior that had orchestrated her PTSD in the first place.

In the dream she saw herself running toward the white van, balloons adorning its side. She slid to a halt at the back of the van, fired three rounds into the lock and yanked open the door. Then Shakey Kunde, the first of Waseem Jarrah's suicide bombers, raised his Glock and a spitfire torrent of gunfire erupted. Jana felt the bullets slam into her chest and she rocked back. Kunde plunged his hand into the metal canister and detonated the nuclear device. The white-hot flash was unbearable. After that, Jana walked among the dead whose flesh fell from their bones. She would scream herself awake.

Her psychologist, Kelly Everson, worked daily with Jana to create a new version of the dream. In this version, Kelly reinforced the truth of that day's actual events; Jana had shot the terrorist to death an instant before he detonated. But Kelly mixed truth with fiction and had Jana imagine her own skin as being as impenetrable as Kevlar. The terrorist's bullets simply bounced off.

As Jana came to grips with the flashbacks, she came to another truth, the realization that she no longer knew herself. So much of her childhood she now knew to be a lie. Her father, a career CIA officer, had committed treason along with her uncle. Jana was the only child of one of the worst spies in US history. She was a child of broken trust.

And her mother, murdered by her father's Russian handlers, gone, gone forever. But the most painful was her grandfather, the one man she had trusted her entire life. He had become her whole world, and yet not even his words could be trusted. He had never told her the truth about her father and uncle and had lied to cover it all up.

Finally there was the self-knowledge that while Cade had risked everything to rescue her, she had chosen the mission over Cade's life. The words of the late Director of the FBI, Stephen Latent, played out in her thoughts. "I chose my career over my wife. I may as well have divorced her the day I took office. Don't make the same mistake." Cade visited the hospital with frequency, but Jana knew that in the jumble of her mind, she would need time and space in order to make sense of it all. She would have to get away from everything in order to find out who she really was. She withdrew, and their relationship fractured.

To this day, the federal government has never disclosed to the American public the truth about what almost happened at the Yellowstone Caldera. Rumors and unverified stories circulate on conspiracy-theory websites about the events that led up to the death of the most wanted terrorist in the world, Waseem Jarrah. But government officials provide no corroboration, and wild theories continue to abound in such circles.

One theory, though, the one proposed by Russian analyst Konstantin Slokovich, has taken on a life of its own. He had first suggested that the United States be taken out in one swift blow by a single nuclear detonation at Wyoming's Yellowstone Caldera. The story gained validity when it was later rumored the US government had permanently relocated radiation-detection sensors to the hillsides surrounding the greater Yellowstone park area.

As the questioning over Rafael's death intensified, Jana Baker applied for, and was granted, a leave of absence from the FBI, the second in her short career. Without telling anyone, she packed a bag and walked into Reagan National Airport. She had no plan, and no destination in mind.

As she studied the list of outbound flights, it occurred to her to fly back to Spain and once again hike the Camino Trail, a place of solace and peace that she would carry inside her for the rest of her days.

But in the end she purchased a one-way ticket to the Caribbean island of Antigua where she rented a small, one-bedroom house on the outskirts of the township of Saint John's.

She took a job at a little tiki hut just off the beach, and much to her pleasure, the hut sold suntan lotion.

A NOTE FROM THE AUTHOR

I've had a lot of readers ask me, how much truth and how much fiction is in *Breach of Protocol*? Well, there's a lot of both contained in the story you just read. But consider these things:

The Yellowstone Caldera—the caldera itself is real, but a supervolcano sleeping underneath? One of the largest active continental volcanic fields in the world?

Does the Russian government believe detonating a nuclear weapon at the caldera would annihilate much of the United States? Is that even possible?

What about the two-mile-deep mine shaft at Parkfield, California? What's the truth behind that?

Tri-methylfentanyl? Was it actually used in by Russian Spetznatz troops as they conducted a raid to save hostages?

Who was the real Aldrich Ames? An American CIA employee turned spy?

How about the Four Horsemen of the Apocalypse? What do the Bible and Koran actually say about these?

And finally, the sword of Al-Battar. Are there really nine swords that belonged to the Prophet Mohammad? Is Al-Battar really said to be the sword Jesus will use when he returns?

As a thank-you for being a reader, all the answers and more are available free. Just visit the author's website at NathanA-Goodman.com/breach/ for an instant download.

Thank you for reading, and as always, you can sign up to be notified of new novels in the Jana Baker Spy-Thriller Series at NathanAGoodman.com/email/

And finally, it would mean a lot to my author career if you would rate Breach of Protocol at the retailer you purchased it from.

Thank you and good reading,

Nathan Goodman, Author

ACKNOWLEDGEMENTS

Special thanks to the following experts, without whom this book would not have been possible: David Bakken, MD and Michele Burns, MD for their thorough review of medical details, the U.S. Geological Survey for providing information used in the geological-related scenes, and the tireless work of my Vermont-based editor, Keith Morrill, who added such value to the story.